Chasing the American Dream

Chasing the American Dream

Polish Americans in Sports

Thomas M. Tarapacki

Hippocrene Books
New York

For information address:
Hippocrene Books
171 Madison Ave.
New York, NY 10016

Library of Congress Cataloging-in-Publication Data
Tarapacki, Thomas M.
      Chasing the American dream : Polish Americans and sports / Thomas M.
Tarapacki.
            p.   cm.
      Includes bibliographical references (p. 143-145) and index.
      ISBN 0-7818-0423-X
      1. Polish American athletes—Biography.   2. Polish Americans—Social
conditions.   I. Title.
GV697.A1T37   1995
796'.092—dc20
[B]   95-39878
                                 CIP

Printed in the United States of America

*To my wife, Mary Ilene, for helping me
chase my dreams.*

CONTENTS

ACKNOWLEDGMENTS

There are many people that I am indebted to for helping me with this book, starting with Mark Kohan, my editor at the *Polish American Journal*, who first suggested the idea of this book. He, Paulette Kulbacki, Sophie Knab, Kathy Sobocinski and the rest of the staff of the *Journal*, were very helpful throughout this effort.

I first became seriously interested in examining the Polish American experience while working for the *Am-Pol Eagle*, Buffalo's Polish American weekly newspaper. The staff there, especially Bob Pacholski, David Rutecki, Renee Harzewski and the late Matthew Pelczynski, guided and inspired me as I sought to learn more about my Polish heritage.

Many people provided me with information and support during the preparation of this book, including George Buksar, Jay Burney, Peter Cava, Henry Dende, Russ Duszak, Dr. Bill Falkowski, Nick Frontczak, Dr. Aleksander Gella, Chuck Hershberger, Don Horkey, Joe Janowski, Buck Jerzy, Stan Kokoska, Ed Muszynski, Ed Pett, Jeff Portko, Jan Wydro, and Fabian Zygaj. Thad Cooke was a frequent source of information and motivation, and Andrew Golebiowski helped me with the translation of Polish language materials.

Much of this book was derived from materials gathered while writing my sports column for the *Polish American Journal*, so the many readers who provided me with information played an important role in the preparation of this book. They include George Findlay, Ed Kwiatkowski, Joseph Kusel, Walter Mysliwczyk, William Naskar, Matt Obloza, Walt Piatek,

Walt Zaneski, and the late John Perkoski.

A number of institutions were very helpful, particularly the National Polish American Sports Hall of Fame and Museum, the National Baseball Library and Archive, the Buffalo and Erie County Public Library, the Buffalo and Erie County Historical Association, and the Polish Falcons of America.

I also owe a great deal to the many sports figures that I interviewed for this book, especially the late Chet Mutryn, a great athlete and a good friend. For me, Chet epitomized the best qualities of the Polish American athlete, combining remarkable athletic ability with hard work, intelligence and humility. He was an outstanding running back for Xavier University and the Buffalo Bills (one publication rated him the greatest running back in the pre-1950s era) and a three-time All-Pro. Although he did not achieve the fame and fortune accorded many modern athletes, Chet was never bitter or angry about being "born too soon." The former Navy lieutenant was a solid citizen who made many contributions to his community, and was a real inspiration to me.

Lastly, I would like to thank my wife, Mary Ilene, for her love, patience and constant encouragement, and my children, Alex and Mariah, for their love and understanding.

FOREWORD

Sports has long played an important, if often unrecognized, role in the evolution of the Polish American community. Through the years, the world of sports and athletics has played a very significant role in the shaping of Polonia.

In many ways, Polish Americans' struggle to succeed on the play fields and in the gyms represented their community's efforts to survive and thrive in American society. The triumphs of great athletes like Stan Musial and Tony Zale not only were tremendous personal accomplishments, but they helped instill great pride, honor and confidence in Polonia.

Sports became a career for many Polish Americans, providing unmatched opportunities for social and economic advancement. But for many others, sports opened the doors to other professions by creating self-confidence, producing educational opportunities, and improving social mobility. One such example was the man who is probably the most popular and respected political leader in my home town of Buffalo, New York. Henry Nowak, the son of a factory worker, developed into a record-setting basketball player at Canisius College. He passed up a pro career to get his law degree, and eventually entered politics. Despite his quiet demeanor, Hank Nowak had extraordinary success and was elected to represent Buffalo in Congress for eight consecutive terms, usually with overwhelming majorities.

But sports benefitted the "average" Polish American as well as the so-called "superstars." It provided convenient and inexpensive recreation accessible in some form to just about everyone. It promoted cooperation and teamwork. It enhanced self-esteem and confidence. It was a fun and healthy activity. In short, sports improved the quality of life for Polish Americans, particularly during the years between the world wars when opportunities were very limited.

As president of the Polish Falcons of America, I am proud of the unique role that my organization played in this regard for over one hundred years. The Falcons promoted sports not just because of their various social, economic and health benefits, but also because they served as a vehicle to promote Polish culture and advance the cause of Polish Americans. As the Polish American community has changed over the years, so too have the Falcons altered their programs to remain a vital part of Polonia and successfully pursue its goals.

In examining the historical development of the Polish American community, it is important to have an understanding of the material as well as the symbolic impact of sports. I hope that this book will lead to a greater recognition that for the Polish American community, sports has certainly been "more than just a game."

—Lawrence R. Wujcikowski
President, Polish Falcons of America

PREFACE

What is a Polish American? Defining ethnicity in this era of increased intermarriage between different ethnic and racial groups in this country can be very difficult these days, and determining Polish heritage can pose some particular problems. It must be remembered that for many years Poland was a commonwealth that included other countries and ethnic groups. In addition, Poland's borders changed throughout its history and even disappeared from the map for over a hundred years—including the period when Polish immigration was at its zenith.

There were sizable ethnic minorities living in Poland, particularly Ukrainians and Lithuanians, with varying degrees of assimilation. Although Polish American commonly means Polish American Catholic, there was also a significant Jewish population in Poland. Most Polish Jews were not fully assimilated into Polish society, with some notable exceptions, and in this country tend to identify as Jews rather than as Poles.

Poles and other Eastern and Central European ethnics were often grouped together, by both themselves and others. The legendary football player Bronko Nagurski was widely considered to be Polish, though both of his parents were Ukrainian. Another football player of a much later era, linebacker Jim Cheyunski, had a name that appeared to be Polish. Fans assumed Cheyunski was Polish, and he never told them that he was really Lithuanian because he enjoyed the adulation from the large Polish American community in Western New York. The paternal grandparents of football great Mike Ditka were Ukrainian and Polish (his maternal grandparents were German and Irish), and both the Ukrainians and the Poles eagerly claim him as one of their own.

In America, many Eastern and Central European ethnics identified with the Poles. I had heard a story about how some of Boston College's top football players had taken to complaining about their coach, Frank Leahy, before the 1941 Cotton Bowl. The players griped in Polish so Leahy could not understand what they were saying, but the coach had a good idea of the subject of their conversation. After a few days Leahy told the players that he had purchased a Polish-English dictionary and would be listening closely to everything they had to say. One of the players mentioned was Mike Holovak. Since that is not a Polish name I wrote to Holovak, who at the time was general manager of the Houston Oilers. He confirmed the story, but added that both of his parents came from Czechoslovakia. That team had many players of Polish descent, he pointed out, such as Chet Gladchuk, Joe Zabilski, Walt Duzinski and Henry Toczylowski and "the players, such as myself, of Slavic origin were included in the Polish group."

Many other Poles and other ethnics either lost track of or never really knew the exact origins of their ancestors. Some only know that their parents came from "the old country."

More recent changes in this country have further clouded ethnic identification. With the increased mixing of ethnic groups, it is not unusual for a person to have each parent descended from two or more distinctly different ethnic groups. Many people with mixed ancestry choose mixed ethnicities. Henry Perez, an Olympic gold medalist in judo, has a Puerto Rican father and a Polish mother and calls himself a "Polarican." Today there is a greater recognition that a person can have multiple ethnicities, just as a person can have multiple identities; for example, a man could be a lawyer, a husband, a father, and a community activist at the same time without having to narrow his identity to just one.

While preparing my regular sports column for the *Polish American Journal* a few years ago, I thought that it might be interesting to prepare an "All-Polish American College Basketball Team." After my feature on the top mens college basketball players of Polish heritage was published, I received a number of inquiries from across the country about the fact that Christian Laettner, the Duke All-American, was not on the squad. Uncertain of his ethnic background, I contacted Bonnie Laettner, the mother of the basketball standout. When I asked whether her son could be considered Polish American, she embarked on a rather extensive examination of both sides of the family tree. Mrs. Laettner's maiden name was Turner, anglicized from Turkowski, and her mother's maiden name was Maliniak, so she always had assumed that her side of the family was Polish. Her pursuit of the full ancestry of both sides of Christian Laettner's family (she also found Polish ancestors on her husband George's side) was made a difficult task by Poland's unique history. Her often disconcerting and confusing search led her to conclude that: "Christian Laettner is as Polish as he wants to be."

We certainly do make conscious choices regarding our ethnicity, but there are factors in our personal historical heritages that we do not control, such as who our parents are. Whether or not we accept our ethnicity or make an effort to maintain an ethnic identity, social scientists recognize that our ethnic background is manifested in our behavior in a number of ways.

It was not the intention of this book to define what constitutes a Polish American, or to produce an in-depth study of ethnicity, or to provide an encyclopedia of every significant athlete, team or contributor in Polish American sports history (though it does cover many of the major Polish American sports figures). The main purpose of this book was to examine the tremendous social, cultural and economic effect that sports had on the lives of Polish Americans. All too often, people view sports as simply "fun and games" and do not recognize how it has affected society. For Polonia (people of Polish heritage living outside Poland), athletics was a force in shaping lives as well as defining the community, and **Chasing the American Dream** is an attempt to assess that impact.

1

INTRODUCTION
From Mines and Mills to
Stadiums and Arenas

In the years following World War II, few Polish Americans were prominent figures in mainstream American life. There were no national leaders of business or industry who were of Polish heritage, no Polish American U.S. Senators or state governors.

In the world of sports, however, Polish Americans were at the center of attention. In 1946 Stan Musial won the National League Most Valuable Player Award, and he and rookie standout Whitey Kurowski led the St. Louis Cardinals to victory in the World Series. Notre Dame's Johnny Lujack and Leon Hart won college football's top honor, the Heisman Trophy, in 1947 and 1949, respectively, and Vic Janowicz of Ohio State won that award in 1950. Tony Zale, "The Man of Steel," reigned as Middleweight Boxing Champion. Frank Parker was one of the top tennis players in the world and was ranked number one in 1948. Future Football Hall of Famer, Alex "The Great" Wojciechowicz, led the Philadelphia Eagles to National Football League championships in 1948 and 1949. All were descendants of Polish immigrants who used sports to overcome a variety of obstacles to their advancement and to attain "The American Dream."

It is believed that Poles first came to the American continent in 1608 as part of the settlement in Jamestown, Virginia. It was not until much later, however, that large numbers of Poles felt compelled to leave their homeland and come to the New World.

Poles were not highly motivated to come to America during the early days of its settlement by Europeans. In the 15th and 16th centuries, Poland was one of the most powerful and influential nations in Europe. Poland had formed a political system called "the democracy of nobles" and was considered a place of great religious and political tolerance.

In the 17th century, Poland began to experience a gradual and irreversible decline, due in large part to the short-sightedness of the ruling nobility. The democratic republic of nobles was slowly transformed as a small group of aristocratic magnates gained control and opposed strong central leadership in order to protect its own interests.

The ruling aristocracy controlled large land holdings, which was the source of their power. They ran their estates through the institution of serfdom, which made the peasants almost slaves of the nobility. The two classes had little in common except for their Catholicism. Traditionally neither class was involved in commerce and trade, which was the domain of ethnic minorities, mostly Jews and Germans.

Poland's very existence was threatened in the mid-18th century by internal instability brought about by the self-serving aristocracy and the rise of powerful neighbors. In 1772 Poland experienced its first partition, as Russia, Prussia and Austria annexed Polish territory. Another partition occurred in 1793, and a third partition in 1795 wiped Poland off the map for more than a century.

Serfdom was eventually abolished at different times in each of the partitioned areas, though it did not significantly improve life for most peasants. While it did give the peasants more freedoms and rights, it also deprived them of security. The abolition of serfdom, combined with new agricultural efficiencies and other far-reaching economic changes, helped create a rural labor surplus. Peasants left the countryside in droves to seek employment in cities. In large part because of the Poles' traditional emphasis on controlling land at the expense of commerce and manufacturing, the Polish industrial economy had been slow in developing and could not support the influx of unskilled workers. Many Poles were forced to leave their homeland *za chlebem*, "for bread."

Prior to 1870 Polish immigration to America had been slow and sporadic. It has been estimated that there were about 30,000 Poles in the United States at the time of the American Civil War. Most were either adventurers or political refugees who had fought in one of the unsuccessful insurrections against the partitioning powers (most notably, Revolutionary War heroes Generals Thaddeus Kosciuszko and Casimir Pulaski). In the second half of the 19th century, the social and economic revolution taking place in Europe turned the trickle of Poles to the United States into a mass migration. From 1870 to 1920 about two million Poles came to America. (Accurate numbers are difficult to determine, since official immigration records from the 19th century listed immigrant's country of origin, not their nationality.) Various developments brought about by World War I, including the re-establishment of an independent Poland, slowed immigration considerably. There were periods of increased emigration of Poles (especially immediately after World War II, when Poland fell under communist domination) but nothing like that which took place around the turn of the century.

The Poles who came here during the mass migration had very little formal education and few skills. They were motivated to come to America by the difficult conditions at home (both economic and political) and enthusiastic stories about life in the new land. Many intended only to earn enough money to return to Poland and buy land. For that reason, and because most had no money to buy land here, most did not enter the enterprise where they had the knowledge and experience: farming. In addition, the Poles were used to a more communal method of farming in which villagers supported each other. Instead, they found work in new industries like steel mills, slaughterhouses and mines. The Polish immigrants tended to settle in the large industrial centers of the northeast and midwest. They flocked to the manufacturing centers like Chicago, Buffalo, Detroit, Pittsburgh, Cleveland and Milwaukee, and the small mining towns of Pennsylvania and Ohio.

Life was difficult for Polish immigrants to this country, particularly the Poles who came to the United States during the mass migration of the late 19th and early 20th centuries. They were mostly peasants who were physically and mentally suited for the unskilled and semi-skilled work in the new industries. Their intellectual capacity was generally never fully tested. Moving up to professional positions in business and other enterprises was difficult, not just because of their own long-held beliefs and behaviors, but also because of the stereotyping and discrimination by others.

Grateful for any work at all, the Poles were more than willing to do the most difficult and dangerous jobs for the lowest wages. True to their peasant origins, they were strong, dedicated, disciplined and submissive workers who were preferred by many employers. (When the Polish workers became organized and aroused, however, they became staunch unionists who were involved in a number of bitter and often violent strikes). The stereotype helped Poles find industrial work, but restricted their upward mobility to better jobs and managerial positions. However, as a group the Poles did not want social or economic mobility but were generally satisfied with well-paying unionized jobs that provided enough income to raise a family and buy a home. In fact, Polish Americans who showed greater ambition were often viewed with suspicion within their community.

Conditions for the Poles were often horrendous, sometimes worse than back in their homeland. They often had to live in simple shacks made with scrap materials outside the mine they worked, or a crowded tenement in the poorest part of the city. Whenever possible they created their own community that contained many of the same elements as their villages in Poland. These communities were usually established around a Catholic church, which had been the traditional gathering place in Poland. Various institutions and services evolved so that residents could attend to most of their day-to-day needs without leaving their enclave. In many cases, they could live in this country for years without ever having to learn the English language.

Most Polish Americans tended to settle in industrial jobs that could provide a steady income rather than risk starting a business or entering a white collar profession, especially when it meant that they had to venture outside their own community. Their peasant culture instilled the Poles with a strong sense of traditionalism and conservativism. For many years they had to deal with landowners, merchants and others who were better educated in business matters and often exploited in such dealings. As a result, they had a profound distrust of other social groups and frequent feelings of inferiority. In addition, almost any change in their village life in Poland had a negative impact, such as war and crop failure. The peasantry therefore placed a high value on maintaining the established patterns of behavior and social structures.

A major disruption occurred during the "Great Depression" between 1929 and 1940, the largest and most severe economic slump in the history of the country. It was estimated that half of the nations industrial workers lost their jobs during this period. The scarcity of jobs, combined with the "anti-foreign" sentiment that was prevalent in the United States following World War I, made life very difficult for Polish Americans.

World War II would bring on a variety of economic and social changes in the country that would have a far-reaching impact on America and Polonia. The end of the the war and subsequent political developments also spurred a period of increased Polish immigrations that also contributed to the ever-changing character of Polonia.

Sometimes for better and sometimes for worse, today's Polonia is dramatically different from the Polonia of fifty years. Polish Americans have slowly moved into the mainstream of American society and now hold positions of responsibility and stature in nearly every enterprise and occupation. They are more confident and assertive, and willing to break with some of the traditional beliefs that hampered them in the past. Yet while Polonia has undergone tremendous changes, it remains a functional and viable community.

Many immigrant groups that did not have a strong tradition of scholarship or did not bring marketable skills with them were drawn to sports and entertainment in the first half of the 20th century. The world of entertainment did not attract a large number of Polish Americans, but many did become intimately involved in sports. Their relationship with athletics was a unique one that had a significant and lasting impact upon the development of Polonia. Sports was an important means through which many Polish immigrants were able to overcome the barriers to their full participation in American society.

2

BASEBALL: THE GREAT (POLISH) AMERICAN PASTIME
From Miners to Majors

Baseball dominated the modern American sports scene from the late 1800s until midway through the 20th century, and for many years was considered "The National Pastime." Young Americans from poor and working-class backgrounds saw the sport as a means to affluence or at least financial security. Young Polish Americans and other ethnics, anxious to become assimilated into American society, also considered the sport as one of the best ways to become "true Americans." Unlike many other professions at that time, baseball was considered by many to be the epitome of the ideals of democracy and equality upon which the nation was founded. The widely held belief of the time was that baseball was one enterprise that any man (unless his skin was black) would be evaluated solely on the basis of his performance on the field, not on where his parents came from or what school he attended.

Through the years, a number of Polish Americans like Stan Musial, Carl Yastrzemski and Phil Niekro have become closely identified with the sport, but the Polish connection with baseball predates even the establishment of the major leagues.

According to historian Artur L. Waldo, Poles were the first to play a form of baseball on the American continent. He traced the game back to the "Polanders" who came to the first English-speaking settlement in Jamestown, Virginia, in the early 1600s. According to historical sources, in October 1608

Carl Yastrzemski watches a long hit go just foul as he tries for his 400th homer at the end of June 1979.

the ship *Mary and Margaret* brought the first Polish settlers to Jamestown: Michal Lowicki, a merchant, Zbigniew Stefanski, a glass-blower, Jan Mala, a soap-maker, Stanislaw Sadowski, a water mill builder, and Jan Bogdan, a shipwright. The Poles were apparently part of a group of craftsmen recruited by Governor John Smith and the Virginia Company to help develop industries in the colony. They are credited with setting up the first glasshouse on the continent and staging the first civil rights strike. Artur Waldo also says that the Poles introduced America's pastime to America.

The Poles, like other Europeans, played various games with sticks and balls centuries before the development of modern American baseball. There were many different versions with varied numbers of bases and configurations of bases. Waldo wrote that the Polish game, known as *pilka palantowa* (meaning "bat ball") or simply *palant*, made its appearance in Poland sometime near the end of the 14th century and became very

24

popular among university students and many adults. He described the game at that time as quite similar to baseball as we know it today, as it was played on a diamond-shaped playfield with eight bases.

The various immigrant groups brought their own versions of bat-and-ball games to this country, and various regional variations evolved and became very popular in the early 1800s. Most baseball historians do not credit any single group or individual with having invented the game, citing the different sources that contributed to the development of the game. They trace the birth of "modern" baseball to 1846, when the New York Knickerbocker baseball club established a set of rules that would soon become the favorite brand of baseball in the northeast. The "New York game" featured nine-member teams with regular line-ups, a playing field with four bases in the shape of a diamond, and the elimination of the common practice of getting a runner out by throwing the ball at him, or "soaking."

The Civil War helped spread the Knickerbockers' brand of baseball to the rest of the country. As America changed from a rural, agrarian society to an urban, industrial one, baseball grew in popularity. Baseball clubs were organized by young professionals like clerks and merchants who wanted an active form of recreation to engage in during their leisure time.

Soon the sport began attracting large numbers of spectators, many of whom were willing to pay admission charges. Professional teams were not uncommon, mostly in the Atlantic states, and some of the players were able to earn more in a baseball season than they did at their regular jobs. At the same time, baseball became less of a fun game and more of an intensely competitive sport.

Polish emigration to the United States at that point had been sporadic and in most part followed failed insurrections. It consisted mostly of political émigrés, who tended to be more educated than subsequent Polish immigrants. One of those political émigrés was Alexander Bielaski, who had fought for Polish independence. Following a failed insurrection, he came to this country and found work in Washington D.C., in the General Land Office. When the American Civil War broke out, he left his position to become an officer in the Union Army, even though he was fifty years old at the time. Captain Bielaski was killed in battle in 1861, leaving behind a wife and seven children.

Despite the tragic loss of his father, son Oscar joined the Union forces as a drummer boy with the 11th New York Cavalry. It was then, the story goes, that Bielaski was taught how to play baseball by Union soldiers during lulls in the fighting.

Bielaski later became a Paymasters Yeoman in the U.S. Navy and after the war, became a clerk in Washington. He continued to play baseball, which was very popular among the young government officials in the nation's capital. He joined the Washington Nationals of the National Association in 1872, appearing in nine games as an outfielder. The following season he played in 38 games for what was then one of the best-known baseball clubs in the country.

When Bielaski started playing baseball, it was a far different sport from the one we know today. None of the players wore gloves of any type. Pitchers were restricted to a side-arm or three-quarter's delivery. A base on balls was awarded to a batter after nine pitches outside the strike zone. Games were played on stone-laden ball fields with rowdy and often abusive fans, or "cranks," harassing the opposing players.

Bielaski was like most of the ballplayers of the era in that he was a young white-collar professional; unlike the others, he was a Polish American. Most ballplayers at that time were of English, Irish or German ancestry.

In 1874 Bielaski joined Baltimore, where he played in 25 games as an outfielder, first baseman and second baseman. The next year Bielaski was recruited to play for the Chicago White Stockings, which owner William Hubert was trying to build into the best team in baseball. He appeared in 52 games as an outfielder.

In 1876, in large part due to Hubert's efforts, the National League was created. It was an effort to have a more centralized, disciplined operation that was controlled by the owners, rather than the players. Hubert's White Stockings, which raided a number of top players from National Association teams, won the first ever National League pennant. Bielaski played outfield in 31 of the 70 games. His batting average was recorded, for the first time, at .206.

Bielaski apparently left the league for a couple of years, then returned for one more season with Washington in 1879 when he hit .336. Bielaski was working for the Navy Department when he dropped dead on the streets of Washington in 1911 at the age of sixty-six.

By the time of Oscar Bielaski's death, some three decades after his playing career ended, there was barely a handful of other Polish Americans who had made their marks in professional baseball. Although tens of thousands of Poles had come to America in those thirty years, very few were involved in professional baseball. Organized baseball no longer attracted mostly college-educated professionals as it had during Bielaski's heyday, but instead drew large numbers of players from lower and working classes. However, Poles and other newer immigrant groups had little presence. Cultural and language barriers certainly made it difficult for these first generation ethnic Americans to enter the profession. Also, the occupations held by most immigrants tended to involve very long hours of hard physical labor that tended to discourage participation in sports. In addition, first-generation immigrants probably did not play the game in their youth and therefore were not likely to have learned baseball's special skills and strategies.

Second-generation Polish Americans became attracted to baseball for a variety of reasons. The areas where most Poles settled, the urban industrial centers of the Northeast, were the regions where baseball was most popular. They were used to and enjoyed physical activity, and playing fields were everywhere. Baseball was an inexpensive sport—all that was needed to play was a bat and ball. As the economic boom following World War I provided the working-class with leisure time, Polish Americans began playing the sport in large numbers.

At the time, other sports were not nearly as appealing or accessible to most Polish Americans. In the early 20th century, football was an elite sport largely played by college students; basketball was still in its formative stages; boxing still had strong criminal overtones; and tennis and golf were elitist upper-class sports played mostly in country clubs. A very important factor in encouraging Polish American participation was the perception of baseball as "the" American sport. By the early 1900s it was already called "The Great American Pastime", and immigrant children viewed it as an avenue to social and economic mobility. It was, for many of them, a way to gain acceptance into American society.

The first known Polish American to follow Oscar Bielaski into the big leagues was named Jack Quinn. He was born John Quinn Paykos, which was anglicized to Picus. Like many Polish American athletes to follow, he was a second-generation Polish American who used sports to escape from hazardous and back-breaking labor in the coal mines of Pennsylvania.

Little is known about the early life of the native of Jeanville, Pennsylvania, but the story goes that he decided to leave the coal mines and pursue a baseball career after surviving a mine fire. Quinn started his major league career in 1908 with the New York Yankees when he was twenty-four years old. He went on to enjoy a long and productive career, playing professional baseball until he was released by the Cincinnati Reds in 1933, shortly after his forty-ninth birthday.

Called "the Methuselah of Baseball" because of his longevity, Quinn holds the distinction of being the oldest regular roster player in major league baseball. He was also the oldest player to hit a home run at age forty-five, the oldest to win a game at age forty-eight, and the oldest to participate in a World Series game at age forty-six.

The 6-ft., 196-lb. righthander compiled a record of 247-217 with a 3.27 ERA during his 23 seasons. He was a steady, durable performer who relied on his low-breaking spitball, which was a legal pitch at the time. Quinn's fitness regime was ahead of his time, as he was one of the few athletes of his era who considered baseball a year-round job. Unlike many of his contemporaries, Quinn gave up smoking, drank alcohol sparingly, and never ate more than two meals a day. He took long hikes through the hills of Pennsylvania prior to spring training to build up his legs for the upcoming season.

There were other Polish Americans who were prominent in the pre-World War I era. Walter "Whitey" Witt, born Ladislaw Waldemar Wittkowski in Orange, Massachusetts, played in the major leagues from 1916 to 1926. He was center fielder and leadoff hitter for the first New York Yankee team to win a World Series in 1923. One of the fastest men in baseball, Witt holds the distinction of having safely bunted six times in one game. He also is remembered as the first Yankee player to come to the plate in Yankee Stadium. "Big Ed" Konetchy, a 6-2, 195-lb. first baseman, was in the major leagues from 1907 to 1921. Playing mostly for the St. Louis Cardinals, the La-Crosse, Wisconsin native posted a .281 career batting average. Anthony "Bunny" Brief (born Anthony Brotzki) played in the majors from 1912 to 1917, but had most of his success in the minors. Twice he led all of the minor leagues in home runs.

Perhaps the most prominent Polish American player before World War I was pitcher Harry Coveleski. (Coveleski's family name was Kowalewski, though he usually spelled it "Coveleskie".) He was called up by the Philadelphia Phillies late in the 1908 season and defeated the contending New York Giants three times in five days. It enabled the Cubs to win the pennant, and earned Harry the nickname, "The Giant Killer," and a $50 bonus. The big righthander later put together consecutive 20-win seasons for Detroit in 1914, 1915 and 1916.

Most of the early Polish American professional baseball players changed their ethnic surnames. Like many Polish Americans, they saw a name change as a way to avoid some of the hostility they often encountered from people who were not Poles or Slavs. This was particularly true in the years following the end of World War I, when widespread "anti-foreigner" sentiment resulted in Congress acting to restrict immigration in the 1920s. Also, many Polish Americans willingly discarded their ethnic names in order to "fit in."

The first great Polish American baseball player was Stan Coveleski, the youngest brother of Harry Coveleski. When he was twelve, Stan left school and started working in the coal mines near Shamokin, Pennsylvania, spending as many as seventy-two hours a week in the mines. He later recalled that the only day he saw the sun was on Sunday, and therefore had very little time to play organized baseball. In the evenings, Stan threw stones at cans he had set up in his yard, and developed quite a reputation for having an accurate arm. That reputation—and his older brothers major league exploits—led a local semi-pro team to recruit him in 1908.

The 178-lb. righthander made it to the majors late in the 1912 season with the Philadelphia A's and posted a 2-1 record in 5 appearances. Despite his impressive performance, the A's were loaded with pitchers, and he was sent down to Spokane in the Northwest League in 1913. The A's later lost Coveleski's rights after a dispute with Spokane, and Stan joined Portland in 1915. It was there that he developed a spitball. The spitball, quite simply, involved putting saliva or other material on the ball to cause it to lose its spin. It was a difficult pitch to master, and its unpredictable path made it hard for catchers to handle.

In 1916 Coveleski moved up to the major leagues again, this time for good, with the Cleveland Indians. He went 15-12 in his initial year with the tribe, displaying the trademark control that produced just 58 walks in 232 innings pitched. Stan rarely attempted to strike out a batter but instead tried to induce the hitter to hit weak grounders to his infielders. He would often retire a side on 3 or 4 pitches. His quick work on the mound and his stoic demeanor earned him the nickname of "The Silent Pole."

Stan helped the Indians improve from 6th to 3rd place in 1917 with a 19-14 record and 1.81 ERA. Brother Harry was then playing in the American League with Detroit, but the

Coveleskis never pitched against each other, steadfastly refusing owners' pleas for a brother vs. brother match-up.

In 1918 Stan hit the 20-win plateau for the first time, posting a 22-13 record and 1.82 ERA for the 2nd-place Indians. The following season he went 23-12, as Cleveland again finished 2nd.

In 1920 Coveleski posted a 24-14 record, and Cleveland won the pennant by two games over Chicago. Stan was the hero when the Indians won the World Series over Brooklyn, five games to none. Coveleski won three games, allowing just 15 hits and two runs in one of the most remarkable pitching performances in postseason history.

For the nation's Polish American community, and Cleveland's sizeable Polonia in particular, Coveleski's World Series heroics in 1920 were exhilarating. Seeing a Polish American succeed in such a high-profile activity—especially since it was "America's national pastime"—produced a great deal of pride. It was particularly gratifying for Polonia because Coveleski seemed to personify those qualities that Polish Americans revered: he was persistent and hard-working but said little and avoided the spotlight.

In 1921 the spitball was outlawed, but Stan was one of 17 spitball pitchers who was "grandfathered" and allowed to continue using it. That year he had his fourth straight 20-win season (23-13), but the Indians narrowly lost the pennant to the Yankees. In 1924, Stan's usually low ERA increased to 4.06, and Indians manager Tris Speaker traded the thirty-four-year-old hurler to Washington. Coveleski bounced back with a league-leading 20-5 record and 2.84 ERA for the pennant-winning Senators. Washington ended up losing the World Series against Pittsburgh, and Stan lost both of his starts despite giving up just 5 runs.

Washington released Stan in 1927. The following year he signed with the Yankees and posted a 5-1 record. In 1929 Stan played semipro ball in South Bend, Indiana, eventually settling there and operating a filling station.

Despite his impressive credentials—including a 214-141

career record and 2.88 ERA—it took forty years for Coveleski to be elected to the Baseball Hall of Fame.

A contemporary of Stan Coveleski who achieved fame was John Grabowski, who caught for the New York Yankees from 1924 to 1931. He caught 68 games for the legendary 1927 New York Yankees, considered by many the best baseball team of all time. Grabowski hardly garnered the kind of attention that was given to stars like Babe Ruth and Lou Gehrig, but he was recognized as a solid contributor. Ford Frick, the future baseball commissioner, wrote in the *New York Evening Journal* in 1927 that the soft-spoken Grabowski "is a good receiver, he has a corking arm, a good head, and he's a fair hitter."

Frick added:

> There's no faster man in the league than little Snuffy Stewart over at Washington. He has tried stealing on Grabowski just once this season—and Johnny tossed him out by a city block. In Philly the other day, Eddie Collins got on first and tried to steal. He never had a chance. Ty Cobb was up next and walked. Ty tried to make second, and Lazzeri [Yankees' second baseman Tony Lazzeri] put the ball on him six feet from the bag. After that, when the A's got on base they stayed there until someone hit 'em around. They took no chances with Grabowski's arm.

But the 1920's was known as the "Era of the Slugger," and one of the best was Aloysius Harry Szymanski, better known as Al Simmons and nicknamed "Bucketfoot Al" because of an unorthodox batting stance.

Born to Polish immigrant parents in Milwaukee in 1903, young Al preferred sports to school. His father insisted that education was the way to get ahead in America, and so Al attended Stevens Point College where he played football. But baseball was his love, and he left college after a year to play for the Milwaukee Brewers of the American Association in 1922. He was a dominant force in the minors and two years later he was called up to the Philadelphia A's.

Al reportedly changed his name to Simmons after being told by a reporter that "Szymanski" would not fit in a box score, and got his new surname from a billboard advertising a hardware company. His Polish heritage was no secret, however, and was often mentioned in articles about him. (After Simmons rose to stardom, *The Sporting News* told of how he bought a big, beautiful house in South Milwaukee for his mother, "Widow Szymanski.").

Al Simmons changed his name, but not the unusual batting stance he developed as a youngster. Although a righthanded hitter, when Simmons would stride, his left foot would point toward third base rather than toward the pitcher. It was generally believed that this tendency, known as hitting "in the bucket," would deprive the batter of power and balance. But not only did it serve Simmons well in the minors, but "Bucketfoot Al" batted .308 with 8 home runs and 102 RBI's as a rookie. After that, purists abandoned their efforts to change his style.

A big man at 6-ft. and 210 pounds, Al nonetheless displayed good speed and was an excellent fielder who twice led the American League in assists. He was an intense player whom sports writers frequently described as a "warrior."

In his second season Simmons hit .384 with 24 HR's and 129 RBI's in 1925, and .343 with 19 HR's and 109 RBI's in 1926. Despite playing in just 106 games in 1927, he hit .392 with 108 RBI's and established himself as one of baseball's great sluggers.

Al was named Most Valuable Player in 1929 (.365, 34 HR's, 157 RBI's) as the A's won the pennant. Philadelphia won the World Series in 5 games over the Cubs, as Al hit .300 with 2 HR's. He was also a key figure in one of the most amazing rallies in Series history. With the A's trailing 8-0 in the 7th inning of game 4, Simmons led off with a home run. He came up again in the inning and singled as the A's scored 10 runs to win the game and, eventually, the series.

The following year Simmons led the A's to another pennant, leading the league in batting average (.381) and runs scored (152), as well as hitting 36 homers and 165 RBI's. The A's won the series in 6 games over the Cardinals, with Al hitting .364 with 2 homers.

During the 1930 season, Simmons suffered a ruptured blood

vessel in his leg during the first game of a crucial double-header. Although he could barely walk, manager Connie Mack sent Simmons up to hit in the second game with Philadelphia trailing 7-3. Al responded with a game-tying grand slam home run that helped the A's win the game.

When the A's wouldn't give Simmons a raise, the stubborn slugger refused to report to spring training in 1931. Hours before the opening game, he finally signed a new three-year, $100,000 deal that was second only to Babe Ruth's contract. Simmons then went out and hit a home run in his first at-bat. He went on to win his second straight batting title with a .390 average, 17 points better than Ruth.

The A's won a third straight pennant that year but lost the series. Simmons, one of the game's great clutch performers, hit .333 with 2 homers.

Al began to develop phlebitis in his leg, and in 1932 he hit .322, his lowest batting average since his rookie year. The A's started selling off their high-priced stars, and Simmons was traded to the Chicago White Sox. He had a couple of good years with the Sox, but his skills had begun to decline. Simmons played for several other teams before returning to Philadelphia in 1944, ending his career just 73 hits short of the coveted 3000-hit mark.

Simmons hit .334 over his career, with 307 home runs and 1,827 RBI's. In his first 11 seasons he never batted less than .308 or had fewer than 102 RBI's.

Simmons coached for a while, and then directed a sandlot baseball program in New York City before returning to Milwaukee. It was there that he suffered a heart attack and died just four days after his 53rd birthday. Three years before his death, Simmons was inducted into the Baseball Hall of Fame. But he received almost as great a tribute when Connie Mack, who managed 7,878 games (more than anyone else in major league history), was asked who would comprise his ideal team. Mack replied, "If I could only have nine players named Al Simmons."

In the pre-World War II era, a few other Polish Americans

made their marks in major league baseball. They included: Frankie Pytlak (1932-46), a small but effective catcher for the Indians and Red Sox, batted over .300 four times; John Mokan (1921-27), a speedy outfielder, had a .291 lifetime batting average with the Pirates and Phillies; and Ollie "The Polish Falcon" Bejma (1934-36, 39), a colorful infielder for the Browns and White Sox.

Around the time of World War II, Polish Americans began to really make their presence felt in the major leagues. Leading the way was Stan Musial, the son of a Polish wiremaker from Donora, Pennsylvania, who became one of the greatest players in baseball history and a revered figure in Polonia.

Musial took to athletics at a young age, and received gymnastic training from the Polish Falcons. Stan credited his tumbling exercises with teaching him how to fall and helping him avoid injuries.

Musial encountered a problem that faced many Polish American baseball players, especially the children of immigrants. Most Polish parents were supportive of athletics but placed a much greater value on a college education. Young men who excelled in football or basketball generally attended college before pursuing a professional career. Until relatively recently, however, most baseball players bypassed college and developed their skills in the minor leagues.

Stan Musial was not only a standout in baseball, but was also an outstanding basketball player. In fact, many thought that it was his best sport. When he was offered a basketball scholarship to the University of Pittsburgh, his father urged him to continue his education. Young Stas (pronounced "Stash") desperately wanted to play pro baseball, and Lukasz Musial eventually—and reluctantly—agreed to let him sign with the St. Louis Cardinals.

"Stas" started out as a pitcher in the St. Louis organization. He was a good enough hitter, however, that he played in the outfield on days when he wasn't pitching. One day in 1940, while playing for Daytona Beach in the Florida State League, Musial dove for a low line drive and caught his spikes in the outfield grass. He injured his left shoulder and, though X-Rays were negative, his throwing was affected.

In 1941 Stan went to Springfield of the Western Association as an outfielder and hit .379 with 26 homers in just 87 games. He was moved up to Rochester of the International League, where he hit .326 in 54 games. Late in 1941, the Cardinals announced that they had purchased the contracts of third baseman George "Whitey" Kurowski, pitcher Hank Gornicki and Musial. The twenty-year-old Musial appeared in a dozen late-season games, hitting .426.

Stas became a regular for the Cards in 1942 and, except for one season in the Navy, he would play for St. Louis for the next twenty-two years. Like Simmons before him, Musial had a distinctive batting stance that was criticized by "purists" early in his career. Musial hit with his bat held high from a coiled crouch that some described as looking like "a little boy peeking around a corner." Also like Simmons, Musial used his unorthodox stance to become one of the greatest hitters in the history of baseball.

The Polish American community rallied around Musial. Although his name was not immediately identifiable as Polish, Musial was openly proud of his Polish heritage. Even Polish American intelligensia and others who tended to hold athletes in low esteem had high regard for Musial. Not only was he a great ballplayer, but he was an extremely popular and highly respected man who was very supportive of Polish American causes.

Stan was inspired to reach the 3000-hit mark by Al Simmons, whom he described as "a particular hero to kids of Polish ancestry." In 1950, Simmons, who had fallen short of the coveted milestone by just 73 hits, encouraged Musial to always "bear down all the way." Some eight years later, on May 13, 1958, Musial reached the 3000-hit plateau in Chicago's Wrigley Field, and a couple of other Polish Americans were involved, as Musial recalled:

The pitcher was a young Pole, Moe Drabowsky, who had me beat on at least one point. He'd actually been born in Poland. When the count reached '2 and 2,' Moe fired a curve ball for the outside corner. I picked up the spin of the pitch, strode into the ball and drove it on a deep line into left field. I knew as soon as it left my bat that it would go between the left fielder, Moose Moryn, and the foul line.

Musial added to that total over the next four years, getting 3,630 hits before he retired. He also collected 475 home runs, 1,956 RBI's, .331 batting average, and numerous records. He had many great years, but perhaps the most remarkable was 1962 when, as a forty-one-year-old grandfather, Musial batted .330 with 19 home runs and 82 RBI's.

Musial was named to the *Sporting News* major league All-Star baseball team 11 times and made the National League All-Star team 24 times. He was named the National League Most Valuable Player three times and finished second in the voting four times.

Baseball fans sometimes forget what a great ballplayer Musial was because he was a genuinely nice person who never seemed to be involved in controversies. As Bill James put it:

> What he was was a *ballplayer*. He didn't spit at fans, he didn't get into fights in nightclubs, he didn't marry anybody famous. He hustled. You look at his career totals of doubles and triples (725 doubles and 177 triples), and they'll remind you of something that was accepted while he was active, and has been largely forgotten since: Stan Musial was one player who always left the batters box on the dead run.

Many other Polish Americans excelled during the post World War II era. As the *Bill James Historical Abstract* noted: "There were probably more Polish players in the fifties than blacks (Kluszewski, Mazeroski, Kubek and Musial were some of the good ones; the Polish population in baseball was at its all-time high)." Nearly every major league team had at least one or two clearly identifiable Polish Americans on its roster.

Ted Kluszewski was known as much for his bulging biceps as his impressive hitting. "Big Klu" was a powerful slugger who averaged 43 home runs and 116 RBI's from 1953 to 1956, yet he had a .298 lifetime batting average and a low strikeout ratio. Very agile despite his muscular frame, beginning in 1951 he led the National League in fielding for five straight years,

Stan Musial was a player who always left the batter's box on a dead run.

a major league record.

Another standout was George "Whitey" Kurowski, a three-time All Star who played third base for the Cardinals from 1941 to 1949. He was probably best-remembered for his dramatic home run that allowed the Cardinals to win the 5th and deciding game of the 1942 World Series against the Yankees. The fact that he played major league baseball itself was quite an accomplishment for the Reading, Pennsylvania native. When Kurowski was eight, he fell off a fence and cut his right arm above the wrist severely. He did not receive proper medical treatment and developed osteomyelitis. A good deal of his ulna bone rotted away, and about three inches of it had to be surgically removed. Despite that injury, he hit .286 over 10 seasons and played on three World Series champions.

Hank Borowy, a son of Polish immigrants from Bloomfield, New Jersey, was the American League Rookie of the Year for the New York Yankees in 1942. He had some great years and had gone 10-5 midway through the 1945 season when he was suddenly sold to the Cubs. He went 11-2 for the rest of the season, leading the league in winning percentage (.846) and ERA (2.14). He pitched for 10 years and had a 108-82 record.

Joe Collins, born Joseph Kollonige, played from 1948 to 1957 for the New York Yankees. Collins did not post spectacular numbers, hitting .256 with 86 home runs, but had the good fortune to play for the powerful New York Yankees. He played in seven World Series, and hit 4 memorable home runs in the fall classic.

Steve Gromek pitched for Cleveland and Detroit from 1941 to 1957, compiling a 123-108 record with a 3.41 ERA. He mainly pitched in relief for the Indians, but started the crucial fourth game of the 1948 World Series against the Braves. The right hander responded with a complete game 2-1 victory. Jackie Robinson had broken baseball's color line just a year earlier and the photograph of Gromek hugging black teammate Larry Doby, who homered in the game, helped the effort to integrate baseball. The Hamtramck native was later traded to Detroit and led the Tigers with 18 wins in 1954.

Eddie (Lopatynski) Lopat started his career with the White Sox in 1944 before joining his hometown Yankees four years later. He was called "Steady Eddie" because of his reliability, and "Junk Man" because of his assortment of slow breaking pitches. After starting with the White Sox in 1944, he was traded to his hometown Yankees in 1948. When the Yanks won World Championships from 1949 to 1953, Lopat averaged 16 wins a year. In 1951 he won a career-high 21, and went on to pitch a pair of complete game victories in the World Series. In 1953 he led the league in ERA (2.42) and winning percentage (.800, 16-4). After ending his playing days in 1955, he served as a manager, coach, general manager and scout.

Casimir "Jim" Konstanty did not stick in the major leagues until he developed a palmball in 1949 at age 32. Pitching in relief for the Philadelphia Phillies in 1950, the bespectacled right hander had 16 wins, 22 saves and 74 appearances, all National League records. Konstanty led the Phillies to the pennant that year and became the first relief pitcher to win the Most Valuable Player award. He started the first game of the World Series, but dropped a 1-0 decision to the Yankees.

Other players of the era included Barney McCosky, Carl Sawatski, Dick Kokos, Stan Lopata, Stan Rojek, Johnny Wyrostek, Ray Narleski, Cass (Kwietniewski) Michaels, Roman "Ray" Semproch, Hank Majeski, Ray Jablonski, Dick Kryhoski, and Bob Borkowski.

The economic prosperity that followed World War II created new opportunities for Polish Americans and other working class Americans to move into white-collar positions. At the same time, the GI Bill helped make a college education more accessible to the middle class. By the decade of the 1960s, Polish Americans were taking advantage of these unprecedented opportunities to move beyond the professions they were traditionally drawn to in large numbers. Polish American participation in major league baseball declined, although it continued to be a visible presence.

The 1960 World Series pitted the powerful New York Yankees against the Pittsburgh Pirates, who had not won a Series since 1925. The Series went to a deciding seventh game in Pittsburgh. With the game tied 9-9 in the bottom of the ninth inning, Pirate second baseman Bill Mazeroski led off against pitcher Ralph Terry. Maz had been hitting well in the Series, having helped the Pirates win Game 1 with a two-run homer and Game 5 with a two-run double. He swung at Terry's second pitch, a high inside fastball, and blasted it over the left field wall in a dramatic moment in baseball history.

Mazeroski played for the Pittsburgh Pirates from 1956 to 1972, and earned the reputation as the greatest defensive second baseman of all time; he set numerous fielding records, and won 8 Gold Gloves for defensive excellence; he was a solid offensive performer; he was one of the top home run hitters among second basemen despite playing in spacious Forbes Field; yet Mazeroski failed to win induction into Baseball's Hall of Fame.

The Yankees bounced back from that upset to win the next World Series, and the 1961 squad is considered one of the greatest teams in baseball history. Two of the regulars on the team were Polish Americans, shortstop Tony Kubek and first baseman Bill "Moose" Skowron.

Although Kubek is better known today as a baseball broadcaster, he was a mainstay of some outstanding Yankee teams in the late 50's and early 60's. Skowron played most of his 14 years with the Yankees. A notorious bad ball hitter, he still managed to hit .300 five times.

Kubek grew up in a Polish neighborhood in Milwaukee and developed into a fine athlete at an early age. That wasn't surprising since his father, as well as three uncles, had played minor league baseball. The elder Kubek quit the sport to support his family, since he could make more money working in a tannery than playing baseball.

Tony joined the Yankees in 1957, earning Rookie of the Year honors by hitting .297 while playing all the infield positions as well as some outfield. The following year, he became the Yankees' regular shortstop for the next eight years. The three-time All-Star played in six World Series during his 9 years with New York. He retired in 1965 at age 29 due to serious back problems.

Skowron, a native of Chicago, replaced another Polish American, Joe Collins, as the Yankees' first baseman. He batted over .300 five times for New York and played in eight World Series. He was the hero of the 1958 World Series, when New York came back from a 3-games-to-1 deficit to beat the Braves. Moose drove home the winning run in Game 6, and hit a three-run homer in Game 7 to give New York a 6-2 win. After playing in his seventh series for the Yanks in 1962, Moose was traded to the Dodgers. Playing against his former club in the 1963 Series, Skowron hit 5-for-13 with a homer as Los Angeles swept New York. Kubek and Skowron were close friends, as Tony noted in his book, *Sixty-One*:

> I think we had a natural empathy for each other because we were both Polish. For us, a big night was going out with Bobby Richardson to the nearest YMCA to play Ping-Pong. Or else Moose and I would stay in the room and play Battleships, the board game.

In 1967 a Polish American named Carl Yastrzemski emerged as one of baseball's biggest stars when he became one of the few players to win the Triple Crown, leading the American League in hitting (.326), home runs (44) and RBI's (121). In doing so, he took the Boston Red Sox to its first pennant in 21 years, still fondly remembered as "the Impossible Dream" season.

But "Captain Carl's" career was one of consistent all-around excellence. When he retired in 1983 after twenty-three years with the Red Sox, Yastrzemski had a .285 batting average, 452 home runs, and 1,844 RBI's. He had won three batting titles, played in 18 All-Star games, and was considered the best defensive left fielder of his era. He was elected to the Baseball Hall of Fame in 1989, his first year of eligibility.

Young Carl was strongly influenced by his Polish-born grandparents. Both came from Poland to the United States at sixteen, married Polish girls at eighteen, and made a living as potato farmers in the Bridgehampton, New York area.

He had many warm memories of growing up in a Polish community: trying unsuccessfully to dance the polka at Polish weddings, eating *czarnina* (duck's blood soup) and other ethnic dishes at Grandma Skonieczny's house, and playing baseball for the Bridgehampton White Eagles.

The White Eagles was a semipro team organized by Carl's father. "Dad was the manager and shortstop, and the rest of the team included Tommy, Chet, Ray and Stan, his four brothers; Mike and Jerry Skonieczny, my mother's brothers; Walter and Leo Jasinski, their cousins; and Alex Borkowski, another cousin," recalled Yaz. The elder Yastrzemski kept the team going into his forties to help groom his son for a major league career.

Yaz dreamed that he would one day follow the footsteps of Polish American baseball stars Stan Musial and Joe Collins. In fact, the batting stance he used for most of his career, with the bat held high above his head, came from emulating Musial.

The elder Yastrzemski only received an eighth grade education, but he insisted that young Carl go to college rather than immediately sign a pro contract after high school. Carl went to Notre Dame on a baseball scholarship, but left early to sign with the Red Sox. His father went along with the decision, but only after securing a promise that Carl would finish his education.

Bill James observed that Yastrzemski and Stan Musial had many similarities besides both being batting champions and excellent fielders. "Both are of Polish descent. Both used very unorthodox batting stances, stances that I would guess an ordinary athlete could not adapt successfully....Each arrived in the majors at the age of twenty-one (Musial had 12 games at age twenty), and each had sudden power surges at the age of twenty-seven."

Despite the pressure of succeeding the legendary Ted Williams as the Red Sox left fielder, Yaz also followed Williams into the Baseball Hall of Fame in 1989, his first year of eligibility.

Other sixties standouts included: Ron Perranoski, an outstanding relief pitcher who earned 179 saves in his 13-year major league career; Dick Tracewski, a reliable utilityman who played on 2 world champions with the Dodgers; and Myron "Moe" Drabowsky, a native of Ozanna, Poland, who pitched from 1959 to 1972. In the seventies and eighties Polish Americans like Tom Paciorek, Richie Zisk, Bob Bailor, Bill Laskey, Frank Tanana, Greg Luzinski and Mike Krukow played on the major league level.

Spanning the sixties, seventies and eighties was the career of Phil Niekro, a righthanded pitcher who played in the majors from 1965 to 1987. Like Stan Musial, he was a uniquely talented athlete who was admired as much for his character as his athletic ability. Like Jack Quinn, he was an effective pitcher into his late forties, finally retiring at age forty-eight. Utilizing the tricky knuckleball pitch, he posted a 318-274 career record. Phil combined with brother Joe for 538 wins, more than any other brother duo in major league history.

The knuckleball is an unusual pitch that few athletes have been able to master. The pitcher digs the fingernails of his first two fingers into the seams of the ball, and then throws it with

In 1987 Phil (left) and Joe Niekro (below) broke the record for pitching wins by brothers. They surpassed the mark of 529 wins set by Gaylord and Jim Perry.

a pushing motion. The ball does not spin and tends to take an erratic and unpredictable path.

Like many other Polish American ballplayers of earlier years, Phil Niekro used baseball to escape from the hard labor of the mines. He grew up in the coal mining region of the Ohio Valley, the grandson of Polish immigrants. His father, Phil Sr., was an outstanding baseball player who had learned the knuckleball so that he could continue pitching after suffering an arm injury. He passed the pitch down to his sons, playing ball with them nearly every day after emerging from the coal mines. "He always had time for us," recalled Phil Jr.

Phil used the knuckleball throughout his high school career. The only game he ever lost at Bridgeport High was a district championship game his freshman year when he faced an opposing pitcher named Bill Mazeroski.

At age 19, Niekro was signed by the Milwaukee (later Atlanta) Braves following an open tryout in 1958. He made the Braves in 1964, but did not earn his first major league win until the following year. He became a consistent winner, but labored in relative anonymity with the struggling Braves franchise. He was widely admired, especially by fans in Atlanta, not just for his unique talent but also because of his loyalty to the franchise and his charitable activities. He posted a 17-4 record in 1982 at age 43, but the Braves unceremoniously released him a year later.

The 45-year-old Niekro signed with the New York Yankees in 1984 and won 16 games. In 1985 he became the thirtieth pitcher to win 300 games on the last day of the season, shutting out the Toronto Blue Jays. He eschewed his usual knuckleball, relying on fastballs, sliders and screwballs until the final batter. At 46, he was the oldest player ever to pitch a shutout.

Playing in New York City, Niekro became a media sensation. He was featured in numerous national publications, many of which emphasized his Polish heritage and his passion for polkas. *People Magazine* wrote: "He is persevering, stoical, fatalistic—a phlegmatic Pole who is a throwback to another generation. He speaks the language of his parents and spends his spare time on the road looking up places where he can dance the polka, work up a good sweat, and drink a few shots and beers with his ethnic compatriots." Niekro told reporters that he got in shape by dancing the polka, and Grammy-winning polka musician Jimmy Sturr, a close friend, recorded the "Hey Niekro! Polka" in his honor. *Sports Illustrated*, in an extensive profile of Niekro, described his knuckleball as "dancing with the sprightliness of a polka step."

Phil's younger brother Joe had some early success as a fastball pitcher, then struggled for a time until he perfected a knuckleball. He was overshadowed for most of his career by Phil, but did accomplish something Phil never did. In 1987, while pitching for the Minnesota Twins, he became the first Niekro to appear in a World Series and was a member of a world championship team.

Phil played for the Indians and Blue Jays before retiring in 1987. He remained active in baseball, including managing the all-female Colorado Silver Bullets baseball team.

In contrast to Phil Niekro's extraordinary longevity, Mark Fidrych only really had one good season. However, his extraordinary talent and unusual personality left an indelible mark on the annals of baseball history.

Fidrych, a 6-foot-3-inch righthander, joined the Detroit Tigers in 1976. Not only was he an exceptional pitcher, but his enthusiastic and sincere approach to baseball was thoroughly refreshing. "The Bird," as he was known, talked to the baseball while he was on the mound, enthusiatically congratulated teammates who made good plays, and generally behaved more like a little leaguer than a major leaguer. Many fans had been turned off by baseball's free agency and escalating salaries, but The Bird's almost child-like approach to the game was reassuring. Mark went 19-9 with a 2.34 ERA in 1976, but he developed arm troubles. He only won 10 more games after his sensational rookie year.

In the late eighties and nineties, standout players like Mark Gubicza, Scott Kaminiecki, Mike Bielecki, John Kruk, Andy Stankiewicz, and Alan Trammell appeared on major league rosters.

Upward mobility to managerial and administrative positions was much slower in coming for Polish Americans than their success on the field. Danny (Ozechowski) Ozark managed the Philadelphia Phillies to three National League Eastern Division titles in the 1970's, and served as San Francisco's interim manager briefly in 1984. Johnny Goryl managed Minnesota from 1980 to 1981. Others, like Rick Stelmaszek, Dick Tracewski and Ron Perranoski, enjoyed long and successful coaching careers. Stan Wasiak became known as "The King of the Minors," managing in baseball for thirty-seven years without ever getting the opportunity to manage in the majors.

One of the few Polish Americans to make a major impact in baseball's front offices was Dave Dombrowski. He was a native of surburban Chicago who played baseball at Western Michigan University, but realized that his future did not lie in playing the game. In 1978 the life-long baseball fan passed up a $52,000 job with an accounting firm to take an $8,000 position with the scouting department of the Chicago White Sox. Blessed with a brilliant mind and a remarkable work ethic, the "Boy Wonder" steadily climbed the corporate ladder. But when his mentor, Chicago GM Roland Hemond was fired in 1986, Dombrowski also was released.

Dombrowski joined the Montreal Expos and became the club's head of player personnel in 1988. Free agency was difficult, especially for a small market Canadian franchise like Montreal, but Dave did such a good job that he was named UPI's Baseball Executive of the Year in 1991.

In 1992 the thirty-five-year-old Dombrowski took on the challenge of heading the Florida Marlins' expansion franchise, which was to begin play the following year. His work in building the Marlins has only enhanced his reputation as one of the best executives in all of baseball.

In Poland, American baseball began gaining in popularity in the 1970's. Although the nation was under communist domination since the end of World War II, Poles felt a close affinity to America and the game which represented the country in their eyes.

A makeshift Polish baseball league took shape, comprised mostly of teams from the industrial region of Silesia. Development of the sport was slow, which was not surprising considering the almost complete absence of everything from equipment to trained coaches.

In 1986, baseball in Poland took an enormous leap forward when a Polish American teacher from Connecticut visited Poland "to see where my dad grew up." While there, Stan Kokoska quickly realized the great interest young Poles had in all things that were American, and baseball in particular. He envisioned Little League baseball not just as a sport for young Poles to play during the summer months, but as a way to build character and foster unity and cooperation among them.

Kokoska talked to Little League headquarters in Williamsport, Pennsylvania, and received an enthusiastic response. He returned to Poland the following year to solicit support from the then-communist government of Poland. Even though many of the fundamental concepts of Little League Baseball were alien to the Poles, Kokoska was able to convince Polish communist officials that Little League Baseball would produce tangible benefits.

The purpose of Little League is not just to teach youngsters baseball skills, but to develop sportsmanship, fair play, leadership and teamwork. The Poles were not used to many of the basic tenets of Little League. For one thing, it is a grassroots effort that involves all youngsters who wish to play, not just the elite athletes. For another, it requires the active participation of volunteer coaches, an unfamiliar practice for most Poles.

With the help of volunteers like Anthony Arnista, progress in establishing the program came very quickly. In July 1989 the Polish Little League was chartered, and Poland became the first "Iron Curtain" country to join the Little League.

It happened that 1989 was also the fiftieth anniversary of the creation of the Little League, and it also was the first year in which a former Little Leaguer was elected to the Baseball Hall of Fame: Carl Yastrzemski. "Yaz," along with other former

President George Bush speaks at ceremonies presenting Poland with a Little League charter. To his right is Stan Kokoska, the Polish American known widely as the "Father of the Polish Little League." (White House)

major leaguers like Stan Musial and Moe Drabowsky, joined the effort to bring Little League Baseball to Europe. Various groups in the United States have raised money and collected supplies to support Polish baseball. The Little League Polish Foundation is now in the process of raising money to construct the Little Leagues European Training Center in Szczecin as the sport continues to thrive in Poland.

If Artur Waldo was correct in his belief that Poles brought baseball to America, the sport has now gone full circle in its successful return to Poland. While it once provided opportunities for young Polish Americans to improve their status, it now provides a means to strengthen cultural ties between the United States and Poland.

3

THE CHICAGO GRABOWSKIS
Polonia and Football

When the Chicago Bears faced the Los Angeles Rams in the 1985 National Football Conference championship game, Bears head coach Mike Ditka referred to his squad as "a Grabowski team" and called the Rams "a Smith team." The point that Ditka was trying to make was that his Bears, who went on to win Super Bowl XX, epitomized tough, determined, aggressive football. His remarks drew on a long-standing stereotype that reflected the prominent role that Polish Americans played in the sport of football.

If baseball provided Polish Americans with their first significant opportunity beyond farms and factories, football helped Polonia define itself. Their dominance in football gave Polish Americans a positive identity in mainstream America and gave Polonia national recognition. In addition, unlike baseball, professional football did not have a system of minor leagues to develop talent. Football players were developed through the colleges, thereby exposing many young Polish American athletes to a new array of educational and social experiences.

American football began to take shape about the time that large numbers of Poles were coming to this country in the late nineteenth century. It developed from various European sports that involved teams of players trying to move a ball across a goal, particularly rugby. The first formal rules were written in 1876. It was a rough and often brutal sport, and

51

Polish Americans were immediately drawn to it. Not only were they well-suited for the rugged physical aspects of football, but the high degree of teamwork and coordination required by the sport was similar to that of the close-knit village community in Poland and the ethnic enclave in America. The very qualities that made Poles excellent industrial workers—durability, persistence, dedication—made them outstanding football players.

In its early days, organized football was mostly played by local athletic clubs and universities. The new Polish immigrants generally did not have the connections to get into the athletic associations; they also did not possess the money (or inclination) to go to college, and that delayed their involvement in the sport. Eventually the sports popularity spread beyond the clubs and colleges, and around the turn of the century semipro teams were sponsored by churches, companies and many small communities. Working-class Americans started to play the sport in significant numbers.

Football grew in popularity in the early part of the twentieth century, and Polish Americans began to display a talent and passion for the sport. In 1904, University of Pennsylvania guard, Frank Piekarski, was named to the All-America team, as Poles and Slavs started playing for many major college teams.

Early in the twentieth century, a number of Polish names began appearing on the roster of the Notre Dame Fighting Irish. Joe Pliska, a 5'10", 180-pound halfback from Chicago, starred for Notre Dame's first undefeated team in 1913. In 1917, another Chicago native who played for the Fighting Irish, 6'1", 224-pound center Frank Rydzewski, earned All-American recognition. Notre Dame was a football power, and soon attained legendary status. Notre Dame football was dominated by Irish Americans in its early days, but in the 1920s and 1930s many Polish and Slavic athletes were becoming "Fighting Irish." Steve Juzwik, Johnny Niemiec, Bernie Witucki, Ralph Jackowski and Stan Chanowicz were just a few. The great Notre Dame Coach, Knute Rockne, once commented: "If I can't pronounce a player's name, he must be good!"

Notre Dame administrators at first discouraged the Fighting Irish nickname but eventually found it preferrable to other unofficial nicknames like "Ramblers" and "Nomads" that implied that its students were always on the road playing football rather than spending time in class. Most athletes who were not of Irish descent took no offense, believing that the nickname represented the team's competitive spirit. The nickname certainly did not discourage Polish American football players from wanting to attend Notre Dame.

For most Polish Americans, higher education was not a priority. It was usually more important for the children to enter the workforce and begin contributing to the family rather than to attend college. Many parents recognized that the only way that their children would be able to really succeed in America would be for them to earn a college degree, but they could not afford the tuition. A football scholarship not only allowed a young Polish American the opportunity to attend college, but it also gave him a sense of status and confidence as a "football hero."

Still, the large White Anglo-Saxon Protestant-controlled institutions of higher learning were intimidating and foreboding to Polish Americans. They felt more comfortable going to Catholic institutions like Boston College, Holy Cross and especially, Notre Dame.

In the 1940s, Polish Americans became a prominent part of Fighting Irish football. Quarterback Johnny (Luczak) Lujack was a two-time All-American (1946-47) and won the Heisman Trophy, given to college football's top player, in 1947. Lujack quarterbacked the Irish to three national championships. Leon Hart (he had a Ukrainian father and a Polish mother named Bartkiewicz) was one of just two linemen to win the Heisman (1949) and twice was an All-American (1948-49). He also played for three national champions at Notre Dame, and later was part of three NFL champions for the Detroit Lions.

Other Notre Dame football standouts of that era included All-Americans quarterback Frank Dancewicz (1945) and

Johnny Lujack enjoyed a brilliant All-American football career at Notre Dame before turning pro with the Chicago Bears in 1948.

tackle Ziggy Czarobski (1947). Lujack, Hart and Czarobski, along with others like Mike Swistowicz, Frank (Trypuczka) Tripucka, Al Zmijewski, Ted Budynkiewicz and Emil Ciechanowicz, were members of the undefeated 1947 national championship team, still regarded by many as one of the greatest college football teams of all time.

That tradition has continued over the years, with Fighting Irish standouts like Bill Wolski, Phil Pozderac, Stan Smagala, Scott Kowalkowski, and Pete Chryplewicz. Ed Rutkowski, the Notre Dame standout of the 1960s, would often joke about his Fighting Irish backfield consisting of Rutkowski, Ratkowski, Perkoski and Lamonica. One of the most famous of the Polish Fighting Irish was Walt Patulski, a 1971 All-American and winner of the Outland Trophy presented to the country's top lineman. Patulski was the first player taken in the NFL draft but his professional career was relatively lackluster because, as one coach put it, "he was too nice a guy."

But not all of the good Polish American football players went to Notre Dame. Leo Raskowski was a standout lineman

Frank Tripucka was an All-American quarterback at Notre Dame and in the NFL. His son Kelly earned All-American honors at Notre Dame in basketball and later starred in the NBA.

for Ohio State in the late 1920s. Guard Ed Molinski was a consensus All-America for Tennesee in 1939. Washington guard Ray Frankowski was All-America in 1941. Halfback "Bullet Bill" Osmanski starred for Holy Cross' undefeated 1937 squad. Ed Brominski starred for Columbia in the 1930s. Eddie Jankowski played at Wisconsin in the 1930s. Center Casimir Myslinski was All-America for the Army in 1943. Ohio State's Vic Janowicz (who went on to play both football and baseball professionally,) won the Heisman Trophy in 1950.

Their ability to play football created new opportunities for many Polish Americans from working class backgrounds, even if they were not All-Americas or Heisman Trophy winners. Not only did they get a chance to attend college, but they were exposed to new experiences that most Polish kids never had. Football was a tough sport, but not as tough as working in the mines and factories, and was often more rewarding.

College football was one of the few areas in which Polish Americans were a visible presence, and before long Polish and football became synonymous.

Playing professional football was an option for many at that time, including Ed Danowski, who quarterbacked the New York Giants to a pair of NFL titles in the 1930s, and Bill Osmanski, who led the NFL in rushing as a Chicago Bear rookie in 1939.

Pro football salaries were not great in the days before television. When the Philadelphia Eagles won the title in 1948, Alex Wojciechowicz, one of their top players and a future Hall of Famer, earned just $7,000.

"Wojie" was the son of Andrew Wojciechowicz, a tailor, and his wife, Anna Chartowicz. Both were Polish immigrants who settled in South River, New Jersey. With English as his second language, school was sometimes difficult for him, but athletics was another story. He was All-State in football and baseball, and also excelled in track and basketball. "Wojie" enrolled at Fordham, where he was a member of the famed "Seven Blocks of Granite" and a two-time All-America. During his three varsity seasons, the Rams lost just three games.

Wojciechowicz was the first draft pick for Detroit in the 1938 NFL draft. The 6-foot, 238-lb. player was an offensive center and a defensive linebacker in the days of one-platoon football. He was an outstanding player who loved the game, and was also able to pursue various business interests off the field.

After several years with Detroit, Wojciechowicz asked to be traded to the east so that he could attend to his business matters. In 1946 Philadelphia Eagles Coach, Greasy Neale, acquired "Alex the Great" and immediately put him next to linebacker Joe Muha in his innovative 5-2-4 defensive alignment. Strong enough to stop the run and quick enough to cover the pass, Wojciechowicz anchored a defense that helped the Eagles win consecutive NFL titles in 1948 and 1949. The Eagles defenders shut out their opponents in both championship games.

The four-time All-Pro retired in 1950 to pursue his real estate career full-time, and helped establish the NFL Alumni Association. He was named to a number of Halls of Fame, including the Pro and College Football Halls of Fame.

Many great players cut short their pro careers, or chose not to play professionally at all, simply because they could not juggle both football and their "real" jobs. Johnny Lujack enjoyed great success with the Chicago Bears but left after a few years for a business career, including operating an insurance agency and automobile dealership. Bill Osmanski entered pro football almost as an afterthought, and also left early to pursue a career as a dentist. Running back Chet Mutryn retired from pro football in 1950 after a five-year playing career to become involved in real estate. As Mutryn pointed out, playing pro football then was not very lucrative, but their sports fame "helped open a lot of doors" for these men in other professions.

Following World War II, the booming postwar economy provided an unprecedented opportunity for economic mobility, and the GI Bill enhanced educational opportunities for veterans. At the same time, the development of television in the 1950s helped popularize the sport and increase salaries. This continued to attract Polish Americans. Frank "Gunner" Gatski emerged from the the coal country of West Virginia by earning a football scholarship to Marshall College. He joined the Cleveland Browns in 1946 and embarked on a career that would put him in the Football Hall of Fame in 1985. The 6-3, 240-pound center was known as "The Silent One" off the field, but on the gridiron he was a dominant and durable presence. His teams played in 11 league championship games during his twelve years as a pro.

Dick "Little Mo" Modzelewski won All-America honors and the Outland Trophy as the nation's best lineman in 1952 for the University of Maryland. The son of a Polish-born coal miner from West Natrona, Pennsylvania, the 6-foot, 235-pound tackle played professionally for fourteen years for four different teams, including a pair of NFL champions—the 1956 New York Giants and the 1964 Cleveland Browns. He was preceded at Maryland by his brother, Ed, known as "Big Mo," a tough fullback who later played professionally for the

Browns. Another pair of brothers, Walt and Lou (Majka) Michaels, came out of Swoyerville in northeastern Pennsylvania to gain football fame. Walt played linebacker for some of the great Cleveland Brown teams of the 1950s, while Lou was an All-American defensive lineman at Kentucky in 1958 and a pro standout as a lineman and kicker. The Browns had a number of Polish Americans, including Chet (Adamczyk) Adams, Jim Ninowski, and Ed Vlinski. Other standouts included Ted Marchibroda, Dick Bielski, Walt Kowalczyk, Ron Drzewiecki and Johnny Olszewski.

In the 1960s Polonia was changing, as Polish Americans were leaving their urban ethnic neighborhoods for the suburbs and taking advantage of new opportunities. As in baseball, the number of Polish American professionals declined but did not disappear. At two positions in particular, quarterback and offensive lineman, Polish Americans were very visible.

The quarterback is one of the most demanding and important positions on a football team, requiring a wide variety of physical and mental skills. Top Polish American quarterbacks of recent years include Ron "The Polish Rifle" Jaworski, Steve Bartkowski, Mike Boryla, Don "Majik" Majkowski, Mike Kruczek, Gary Kubiak, Mike Tomczak and Mark Rypien. (It should also be noted that two of the greatest quarterbacks of all time, Joe Montana and Dan Marino, have Polish blood.

The need to understand blocking schemes and recognize defensive formations makes the offensive line positions among the most challenging in the game. A great deal of discipline is also required, as well as the obvious physical requirements. In recent years, Mark Stepnoski and Steve Wisniewski have earned All-Pro honors on a regular basis. Other top NFL linemen are Mike Munchak, Jim Dombrowski, Bruce Kozerski, Bob Kowalkowski, and Bob Skoronski.

In the 1970s, over a period of four years, three Polish Americans were the first players selected in the NFL draft: Notre Dame defensive end Walt Patulski (Buffalo, 1972), Tampa defensive end John Matuszak (Houston, 1973) and California quarterback Steve Bartkowski (Atlanta, 1975).

By that time, pro football had not only surpassed college football in popularity, it even supplanted baseball as America's most popular sport. Other top Polish American players included Jack Ham, the Hall of Fame Pittsburgh Steeler proclaimed by Polish fans as *Dobre Shunka*, (sic) "Good Ham"; defensive lineman John Banaszak, Danny Abramowicz, who led the NFL in receiving for the New Orleans Saints in 1969; and Chester Marcol, the Polish-born placekicker who became the first player to lead the NFL in scoring on kicking alone.

Like many Polish American football greats before him, Joe Klecko emerged from a small blue-collar town in Pennsylvania to achieve fame on the gridiron. Unlike many of them, playing football was not a way to escape difficult conditions but rather the fulfillment of a dream.

Klecko played most of his career for the New York Jets, and was 1981 NFL Defensive Player of the Year. He was also the first man to earn All-Pro recognition at three different positions: end, tackle and nose tackle.

Klecko grew up in Chester, Pennsylvania and much of his family's life centered around the local Polish parish, St. Hedwig's. Joe Sr., the son of Polish immigrants, was a fine athlete who left school during the depression and held a variety of jobs, including working in a shipyard and driving a truck. He remained involved in sports throughout his life and was a dedicated Philadelphia Eagles fan.

Joe Jr. shared his father's enthusiasm for sports and dislike of school. He was exceptionally stong—Joe could bend quarters with his hands—but Klecko did not get very involved in school sports. He played briefly for the football team at St. James High School, but preferred sandlot sports. That left him more time to earn money working at his cousin's garage, which he did since he was 11. Klecko's abbreviated high school career did not excite college recruiters, and he got a job driving a truck. After a couple of years, Joe was recruited by the semipro Ashton Knights. He was not interested in college, but was registered to play as "Jim Jones" to protect his eligibility. The 19-year-old Klecko more than held his own with an amazing combination of strength and speed and was convinced that he could make it to the NFL if he played college ball. Joe was content with his lifestyle but eventually agreed to attend Temple on a football scholarship. As in high school, he seemed to lack motivation and had an inconsistent career.

He had hoped the Eagles would draft him, but Klecko was picked by the New York Jets in the sixth round in 1977. In his college days, he was clearly physically superior to his opponents, but Joe realized that he would have to work hard to make it in the NFL. He started his first season playing just in passing situations, but by the end of the year he was a starter and lead rookie with 8 sacks.

Klecko played most of his career for Walt Michaels, who also came from working class Polish American roots in a small Pennsylvania town. "I'm a hard-headed Polack just like Walt, and there's a very strong bond in that," said Klecko. Michaels, a former All-Pro linebacker for the Cleveland Browns, was a defensive assistant for the Jets team that won Super Bowl III.

Klecko's tremendous strength and quickness, combined with a fierce competitiveness, made him one of the NFL's top defensive linemen by his second season. The Jets' defensive line became one of the best pass rushing units in NFL history, known as "The New York Sack Exchange," and New York emerged as a contender.

Joe was a popular player who received much attention. He even got small roles in some Burt Reynolds' movies. In *Smokey and the Bandit II*, he played an angry truck driver who, with his bare hand, crushes the badge of the sheriff played by Jackie Gleason. Klecko is listed in the credits as playing a "Polish truck driver." True to form, Joe disdained the Hollywood scene but made many friends among the movies' stunt men.

One time, a radio personality and his producer showed up at a Jets' postgame party. What followed was recalled in *Nose To Nose*, the book Klecko co-authored: "The producer, beer can in hand, proceeded to tell a Polish joke to Klecko, apparently not realizing that Klecko is as Polish as it gets. Klecko gently wrapped his hand around the one the producer was using to

Hank Stram started his head coaching career in 1960 with the Dallas Texans of the old American Football League. With 131 victories, he had a reputation as a great innovator.

hold the almost-full can of beer and squeezed it until the can was flat."

Klecko was eventually slowed by injuries to both knees, which he struggled valiantly to overcome. He ended his career with the Indianapolis Colts in 1988.

Hank Stram did not play pro football, but he did become one of the few Polish American head coaches in the game. Stram was a very successful coach, compiling 131 career victories, winning AFL and NFL championships, and earning a reputation as one of the game's great innovators.

Stram's father was a Polish immigrant who one day challenged the Barnum & Bailey wrestling champion and defeated him. The circus signed the victor as their new champ and he traveled with the show, somewhere changing his name from

Wilczek to Stram. He eventually settled in Gary, Indiana and became a clothing salesman, but continued his strong interest in sports which he passed on to his son. Young Hank was also encouraged to participate in athletics by another Gary native, Tony (Zaleski) Zale.

Hank was only 5 feet 7 inches tall but he lettered in football, basketball, track and baseball in high school. The All-State halfback earned a scholarship to Purdue, and after graduation became an assistant coach at Purdue, making some extra money by playing semi-pro baseball. He later coached at Southern Methodist University, but was passed over for the head coaching job because he was told he was Catholic. Ironically, Stram was then recruited by Notre Dame, and he helped turn around a Fighting Irish team that had a 2-8 season, its worst year ever. Notre Dame had 7-3 and 6-4 seasons while Hank coached there, but head coach Terry Brennan and his entire staff was fired. Hank then coached at the University of Miami until he got a call from Lamar Hunt, the owner of the Dallas Texans of the new American Football League that was beginning play in 1960. Hunt, who had played football at SMU, heard good things about the bright young coach and offered the little-known Stram the head coaching job. Stram took a chance on the fledging league, holding out for $20,000— more than double his previous salary.

Stram epitomized the AFL's fresh, innovative approach to the pro game. An offensive mastermind, he led the Texans to a championship in the league's second season. The team moved to Kansas City and became the Chiefs. On January 1, 1967, the Chiefs defeated the two-time AFL champion Buffalo Bills to earn the right to play in the first season AFL-NFL championship, later to become known as "The Super Bowl." The Chiefs were soundly defeated by the Green Bay Packers, but Stram immediately set about rebuilding the team. Kansas City won the AFL title again in 1969, the final year of the league's existence. The Chiefs returned to the Super Bowl as 13-point underdogs but defeated the Minnesota Vikings 23-7.

Stram left the Chiefs and coached the New Orleans Saints

before embarking on a new career in 1975—broadcasting. He quickly became one of the most popular and highly regarded football commentators, well-known for his uncanny ability to predict plays.

Hank Stram will long be remembered as a winner and one of the game's great innovators. The four-time Coach of the Year pioneered the use of such tactics as the moving pocket, the I-formation, the double tight end alignment and the zone defense. He also installed pro football's first black middle linebacker, Willie Lanier.

Another fine Polish American head coach was Ted Marchibroda. A top collegiate quarterback, he led the nation in total offense for the University of Detroit in 1952. The Pennsylvania native was a first round pick of the Pittsburgh Steelers, playing in the NFL for four years before becoming a coach. After serving as an assistant with the Washington Redskins and Los Angeles Rams, he got the chance to be a head coach in 1975 with the Baltimore Colts. Marchibroda earned Coach of the Year honors as the Colts became the first NFL team to go from last to first in its division in one season.

Marchibroda won division titles in his first three seasons but was fired after consecutive 5-11 seasons. He had no trouble finding work as an NFL assistant. In 1987 he was hired by Buffalo, and assembled an offense that turned the Bills into an NFL power. His quick-striking "no-huddle offense" was one of the most productive in league history.

In 1992, Marchibroda returned to the Colts as head coach, taking over a team (which had since moved to Indianapolis) that had a 1-15 record the season before. He again engineered a dramatic turnaround, as the Colts finished the year at 9-7.

While there have been a number of top Polish American assistant coaches in the pro ranks—including Zeke Bratkowski, Dick Modzelewski, Danny Abramowicz, and Bob Bratkowski (Zeke's son)—there have been relatively few Polish Americans as head coaches in the sport.

Dick Szymanski was one of the few Polish Americans to succeed in the pro football's front offices. The Toledo, Ohio native had an outstanding playing career, playing on championship teams for Notre Dame and the Baltimore Colts. After his retirement, he joined the front office of the Colts, holding such positions as offensive line coach and director of player personnel. In 1977 Szymanski became general manager of the team, a position he held until he was fired in 1982. He went on to scout for the Atlanta Falcons and later served as executive director of the NFL Alumni Association.

A variety of other professional opportunities have opened up in the sport. For example, Eddie Abramowski, an Erie, Pennsylvania native whose promising football career was ended by a knee injury at Purdue, stayed in the sport by becoming a trainer. He has been the Buffalo Bills' head trainer since 1960, and was inducted into the National Athletic Trainers Hall of Fame in 1987.

In college football there has also been a scarcity of Polish Americans heading programs. A few include: Joe Restic, who led Harvard to five Ivy League titles in the 1970's and 1980's; Mickey Kwiatkowski, the architect of one of the country's top Division III programs at Hofstra; and Frank Kush, who posted a remarkable 176-54-1 record at Arizona State and also coached in the pros. Cas Myslinski was athletic director at the University of Pittsburgh from 1968 to 1982, and the Panthers won the national football championship in 1976 under his guidance.

Chet Gladchuk Jr. is one of a new breed of Polish American sports stars. Like his father, a legendary football star at Boston College, he also excelled on the gridiron. But after graduating with a BA in business administration in 1973, Chet earned a masters in sports administration from the University of Massachusetts-Amherst. He then embarked on a sports administration career that saw him return to his alma mater in 1990 as athletic director. He has been credited with revitalizing the Division I intercollegiate athletic program for men and women at Boston College, which is one of the largest in the nation.

When Dick Modzelewski was inducted into the Polish American Sports Hall of Fame in 1986, he articulated what football meant for many Polish Americans, and why so many excelled at the sport:

> "If you've ever worked in a coal mine, you know it's awfully tough work. Thirty out of thirty-three years my dad was known as the champion coal holder of the Alleghany-Ludlum Steel, Coke and Coal Company. He had a lot of desire. I remember one time in particular he came home and he had a hole in his back from battery acid. You could put a finger in it. He should have gone to the hospital or to the doctors, but he went to work the next day. So, he sort of played with pain. He's the guy that gave me all this. Never give up....There were times in those ballgames you get the feeling in your system, well, maybe you're going to lose, maybe I ought to settle down just a bit or just forget it. I always remember his voice coming back saying, 'Don't give up.'....and I coach the Polish way—I coach my players to be determined to win, to have the desire to win."

Many of the qualities that made Polish Americans such proficient industrial workers helped make them outstanding football players, including their physical and mental toughness, discipline, determination, willingness to accept authority, and willingness to make individual sacrifices for the good of the group.

Football has enabled countless working class Polish Americans to attend college and pursue opportunities not normally available to them. Perhaps even more significantly, it gave Polonia a sense of identity and gave Polish Americans status in American society.

4

PUNCHING THEIR WAY TO IMMORTALITY
Stan Ketchel and Tony Zale

Two of the most significant figures in Polish American sports were a pair of middleweight boxers who, other than their success in the ring, had very little in common. Stan Ketchel was a fast-living brawler who was killed at age 24, while Tony Zale was a stoic, dignified man who refused to drink alcohol or smoke cigarettes. Yet both men were sons of Polish immigrants who fought their way to the World Middleweight Boxing Championship and achieved sports immortality.

Stanley Ketchel was born Stanislaw Kiecal on September 14, 1886, in Grand Rapids, Michigan. His father had immigrated to the United States from Prussian Poland. His mother, the former Julia Oblinski, was born in Grand Rapids of Polish parents.

Young Stan was raised in Grand Rapids, but at an early age he began longing for a life of adventure in the American "Wild West." At the age of 15, he hopped a train to Butte, Montana, and found work as a bellhop at the Copper Queen Hotel. One day, he was carrying a tray of dishes when the hotel bouncer tripped him to the floor. Never afraid of a fight, Stan attacked the bouncer and gave him such a beating that the hotel manager hired him as the new bouncer. To make extra money, the teenager would fight all challengers for twenty-dollars-a-week at the Casino Theater. He was not big and never had any boxing lessons, but Ketchel had power in both hands and

Stan Ketchel achieved sports immortality in middleweight boxing.

fought with such intensity, that it appeared he actually wanted to kill every man he fought.

His remarkable success at the Casino—Ketchel once estimated that he vanquished 250 foes there—convinced him that knocking men unconscious was a pretty easy way for him to earn a living. He launched his professional career in 1903 at the age of 16. The young middleweight knocked out his first opponent, Kid Tracy, in the first round and went on to knock out 35 of his first 40 opponents.

Early in his career, an ex-boxer named "Socker" Flanagan told the young fighter to change his name from "Kiecal" to "Ketchel" so that it would be easier for fight fans to pronounce.

One writer described Ketchel as having "a strong, clean-cut Polish face." He was 5-feet-9, 154 pounds, and had blondish hair and blue-green eyes. He was known as a prankster who loved excitement. The colorful fighter usually wore cowboy boots and hat and was rarely without his blue-barrelled revolver. When he was boxing, Ketchel was the vicious

"Michigan Assassin," but outside the ring, he was fun-loving and playful.

The middleweight title was vacant in 1907, and Ketchel went to California to take on the top contenders. When he beat Mike "Twin" Sullivan in February 1908, the 21-year-old fighter won international recognition as the middleweight champion of the world. "When I got to be champ, the old man couldn't have been more pleased if I had been made president of the United States," recalled Ketchel.

As champion, Ketchel fought all of the best fighters in his class, even the black fighters that many white boxers avoided. "A man's color doesn't denote the quality of his punch," he once said.

In September 1908 he lost his title in a controversial fight against Billy Papke, a tough German American with a reputation as a dirty fighter. When Ketchel approached him for the customary handshake to start the bout, Papke floored him. Ketchel, on the canvas for the first time in his career, struggled to his feet. He never really recovered, losing in the 12th round. The pair had a rematch two months later, but there was no handshake. Ketchel battered Papke before knocking him out in the 11th round. Ring observers believed that Ketchel could have put away his opponent earlier, but wanted to punish him for Papke's earlier treachery. Stan became the first man ever to regain the middleweight title.

Ketchel frequently took on heavier fighters and once knocked out light heavyweight champion Jack O'Brien in three rounds. He even challenged Jack Johnson, the heavyweight champion of the world who outweighed the middleweight by 35 pounds. Most heavyweight contenders considered Johnson unbeatable and would not fight the first black heavyweight champion, though much of the public clamored for a "Great White Hope" to "wipe the golden smile" from Johnson's face. Ketchel harbored no racial animosity toward Johnson, but simply viewed the fight as a challenge that he was convinced he would win.

The men fought in Colma, California in 1909, and Ketchel

was the aggressor throughout the fight. Johnson used his defensive skills to avoid Ketchel's powerful punch until he was floored by a sweeping right in the 12th round. Johnson got up and angrily went after his opponent, hitting Ketchel in the jaw with a thunderous uppercut that sent both men sprawling. As Johnson rose to his feet, Ketchel was counted out. In his dressing room, Johnson removed some of Ketchel's teeth that had embedded in his gloves.

Johnson was magnanimous after the fight, saying that Ketchel "has given me a sorer chin than I ever had before." Stan did not accept the loss easily, however, insisting that "but not for that one blow I'd have beaten him."

Despite the loss, Ketchel's remarkable performance solidified his status as a boxing legend. It also convinced many that the heavyweight champion was not invincible. However, Johnson would not lose his title until 1915 when, at at age 37, he was finally defeated by 6'6", 240-pound Jess Willard.

Ketchel and Johnson remained on good terms, and in his autobiography, Johnson wrote that "Ketchel was an excellent fighter in the ring and a fine fellow out of the ring. I admired him and counted him as one of my valued friends."

Late in 1910, Ketchel went to a ranch in Conway, Missouri, owned by his last manager, Pete Dickerson, to train for his next bout far away from the distractions of big city life. On the morning of October 15th, while eating breakfast at the cookhouse, Ketchel was shot in the back with a .22 caliber rifle by a hired hand named Walter Dipley. Ketchel died shortly afterwards in a nearby hospital.

When told the news, Ketchel's friend, Wilson Minzer said: "Start counting now, because he'll get up at nine."

Stories circulated that Ketchel was shot "by an irate husband" for flirting with the cook, Goldie Smith, a story that persists today. In fact, Dipley and Smith were apprehended and charged with conspiring to kill and rob Ketchel, who always carried large amounts of cash with him. Dipley was convicted of robbery and murder and sentenced to life in prison (he served twenty-five years); Smith was convicted of aiding and abetting the crime and was sentenced to twenty years in jail. (She served twelve.)

Despite the rumors about the murder, there was a huge outpouring of affection for Ketchel when his body was returned to Grand Rapids. A crowd estimated at 8,000 crowded St. Adalbert's Church for the funeral, and thousands participated in the procession to the Polish Catholic Cemetery.

In 1994, an official city historical marker commemorating Ketchel was placed in the fighter's hometown, thanks largely to the efforts of local attorney Jeff Portko and the Polish Heritage Society. The marker is located near Ketchel's birthplace in the vicinity of the St. Adalbert's Polish Basilica and School, which he attended. It came about despite the protests of some who questioned whether such an honor should go to someone who led such a fast life and died such an untimely death.

"That attitude toward Ketchel represents an anti-Polish attitude," said Portko. "It's like, 'Oh, that Polish guy, look, he went and got himself killed. Isn't that too bad.'" Portko added that the response of the Polish American community at this funeral was evidence of the admiration they had for their native son. "He was so very important to the Polanders," he maintained. "They were new here, their English was not very good, they were Catholics in a Protestant area, and they were from Eastern Europe and everyone regarded Eastern Europe as backwards in some way. They were proud of Ketchel."

Ketchel was certainly the first Polish American sports superstar (though that term was not yet in use), and his boxing exploits meant a great deal to the large number of Polish immigrants who were settling in this country at that time.

*   *   *

Some thirty years later, another Polish American captured the middleweight title on his way to boxing immortality.

Anthony Zaleski was born to Polish immigrant parents on May 29, 1913, in Gary, Indiana. When Tony was two years old and sick with the measles, his father, a steel worker, went to the drug store for some medicine. As he pedaled his bicycle, he was hit by a car and killed. Tony's mother, six months pregnant at the time, was left with no insurance money and a family of six to support. She had only five dollars after funeral expenses were paid and did whatever kind of work was available to support the family. She even bought a cow to ensure an inexpensive supply of milk for the children. "She was some woman," said Zale. "She gave me my determination."

The Zaleski boys went to work in Gary's steel mills to support the family, and in their free time took up boxing. Following the lead of his older brothers, young Tony went to the gym around age twelve. He won the welterweight class in the Indiana Golden Gloves in 1931, and three years later left his job in a steel mill to pursue a professional career, finding it easier than working in the mills.

Fighting as Tony Zale, he suffered some injuries and gave up the ring after about a year. After two years he was convinced to try boxing again. Now a middleweight at 5-foot -8-inches, 160 pounds, Tony eventually emerged as a top contender. He became known as the "Man of Steel" because of his blue collar origins and his rugged physique. He was known as a vicious body puncher thanks, he said, to his mother: One day he went to the gym after eating one of his mothers big home-made Polish dinners. After being hit solidly in the stomach, he vomitted his dinner and resolved that "I was going to be the one who hit other people in the body."

In 1940, Zale earned a fight against National Boxing Association Middleweight Champion Al Hostak, a Czech from Minneapolis. Zale knocked out Hostak in the 13th round, and then knocked him out again in a rematch. When Zale won a decision over Georgie Abrams in New York City's Madison Square Garden in November 1941, he was regarded as the World's Undisputed Middleweight Champion.

Middleweight champion Rocky Graziano takes a right in the ribs from Tony Zale in their third bout in June 1948.

In 1942, Zale joined the Navy as a physical training instructor at the Great Lakes Training Station near Chicago, and his title was "frozen" until his return. His manager urged him to continue to fight professionally during that time, both to earn some money and to maintain his skills. Zale refused, saying it would not be proper for him to earn big purses while fellow servicemen were risking their lives.

When Zale came out of the service at the end of the war, a colorful young challenger appeared ready to take his title. Rocky Graziano attracted much attention with his record of 32 knockouts in 54 fights. His intense, brawling style led many to refer to Graziano as "the new Stanley Ketchel."

It was a fascinating matchup: Zale was a Pole from the steel mills of the Midwest; Graziano was an Italian from the streets of Brooklyn; Zale was a tough bodypuncher; Graziano was a free-swinging "head-hunter;" Zale was a clean-living Navy veteran who eschewed alcohol; Graziano was an army deserter who spent time in prison; Zale was quiet and shy; Graziano was a colorful, streetwise character.

In the fall of 1946, some 40,000 fight fans filled New York's Yankee Stadium to see whether the thirty-three-year-old "Man of Steel" could withstand the heavily favored Graziano's vicious punches. The crowd was stunned when Zale flattened the twenty-four-year-old challenger in the middle of the first round. Graziano got up and attacked with savage fury, and floored the champion in the second round. For the next three rounds the pair battered each other relentlessly, with Zale suffering a broken right thumb in the process. In the sixth round, Zale drove his broken hand into Graziano's stomach and followed up with a sweeping left hook to the head that put the challenger down for the count. "Clean living did it," said an exhausted Zale.

As Graziano put it, the bout was more a "private war" than a boxing match. Although boxing had declined in popularity during the war years, the intensity of the Zale-Graziano fight renewed interest in the sport. The public demanded a rematch, and the pair fought again almost a year later in Chicago Stadium. Zale again took an early lead but seemed to tire in the 105 degree heat. By the sixth round, Graziano was hitting Zale with a savage fury, but the champion clung to the ropes and refused to go down. The referee stopped the bout and Rocky was the champion.

In June 1948, they met again in Newark, New Jersey. Again it was an all-out war between the two men, but in the third round a powerful left hook by Zale ended the bout. He became the first middleweight to regain the title since Stan Ketchel did it forty years earlier.

The Zale-Graziano bouts, which took place within a period of twenty-one months, are still considered by many the most exciting series of fights in boxing history.

Just three months later the thirty-five-year-old champion, not quite recovered from the punishing series with Graziano, lost his title to Marcel Cerdan of France and then retired. True to his word, he rejected repeated attempts to get him back into the ring.

Ironically, in later years Graziano became even more famous, as Paul Newman portrayed him in the movie about his life (*Sombody Up There Likes Me*) and as Rocky made numerous TV appearances.

Zale led a much quieter life and spent much time teaching youngsters to box. The *Los Angeles Herald Examiner* wrote: "What endures for Zale is the notion of what a fighter's life should be—excess only in work, adherence to regimen, sacrifice, stoicism."

Although the sport of boxing did not contribute a great deal to Polonia's social and economic advancement, the triumphs of men like Ketchel and Zale had great significance in the Polish American community. Their individual bouts in the ring symbolized Polonia's struggle for survival in America, and their victories in this primal and violent sport had a great deal of symbolic value for a community that was fighting its own battle to gain acceptance in American society.

5

FROM HOCKEY PUCKS TO HORSESHOES

Polish Americans had a significant presence in the sports of football and baseball, but there were other sports which they participated in. In fact, there are few sports which Polonia has not impacted in the 20th century.

*   *   *

Relatively few Polish Americans have become prominent in the field of stock car racing, a sport dominated by southern "good ol' boys." But one of the great figures in the history of stock car racing was a Polish American from Wisconsin who died tragically before the age of forty.

Alan Kulwicki suffered tragedy early in life, losing his mother to leukemia and an older brother who suffered from hemophilia. Raised by his father, he graduated from the University of Wisconsin, Milwaukee, in 1977 with a degree in mechanical engineering. Jerry Kulwicki, mindful of the difficulties and dangers of auto racing, tried to discourage his son from entering the sport. Nevertheless, Alan decided that he wanted a career in racing and began racing on local dirt tracks. In 1985, he made his way up to the NASCAR circuit and won Rookie of the Year honors.

A college-educated Polish American from north of the Mason-Dixon line, Kulwicki was a rarity in NASCAR. He was a quiet and hard-working bachelor who was not disliked, but did not really fit in either. When he won his first race at Phoenix in 1988 and celebrated with his backward "Polish victory lap," the veterans on the tour started taking a liking to "Kwikie." He got offers to race for the major teams, but Alan wanted to win "his way"—by driving for a team that he also owned. That had only been done in recent years by Richard Petty, who was backed by family-owned Petty Enterprises.

Kulwicki was deeply involved in every aspect of the operation, from repairing his car to negotiating contracts. In 1991 he attracted a major sponsor, Hooters Restaurant chain, and he finally had some financial stability. His dream came true in 1992 when he won the NASCAR Winston Cup Championship by outpointing Bill Elliott for the season. The victory earned him an additional one million, and the respect and admiration of the racing world. He served to inspire another young Polish American racer, Joe Nemechek, to make it to the NASCAR circuit.

Soon after the Winston Cup title, Kulwicki was back at work, trying to disprove critics who insisted that he would never repeat the impossible the following year. In April 1993, he was flying in a private plane to a race in Bristol, Tennesee, when the aircraft crashed into a hill as it made its final approach. Kulwicki and the other three people on board died.

Alan Kulwicki's life was short—he was only 38 years old when he died—but his remarkable accomplishments made him an auto racing legend.

*   *   *

Walt Zembriski is one of the best golfers on the seniors tour, one of the few who did not play on the regular PGA tour. Still, he is one of the most popular players on the circuit, with a large following of Polish American fans known as "the Warsaw Pack."

Zembriski grew up in a Polish neighborhood in Mahwah, New Jersey. He got his love of golf from his father, a foundry worker who had once caddied for Babe Ruth. Walt practiced with the twenty-five dollar clubs his father brought home, hitting rocks in local sandpits. At thirty-one, he won the match-play final of the New Jersey Amateur, but failed in his efforts to make the pro tour. He continued to play in regional tournaments while making a living as a steelworker.

He eventually moved to Florida, where he could practice his golf year-round. Walt prepared himself for 1985, when he would turn fifty years old and become eligible for the seniors tour. With his union card in his wallet and his mother's rosary in his pocket, Zembriski quickly established himself on the tour. Called "a scrapper, a player of great endurance" by Arnold Palmer, Zembriski was perhaps the best player on the senior tour without previous tour experience.

Other golf champions were Ed Furgol, a seventeen-year pro despite a childhood accident that resulted in a left arm that was virtually useless, and Bob (Algustoski) Toski, a top pro who became a highly regarded golf instructor and author.

*   *   *

Frank Parker of Milwaukee—born Frank Pajkowski—was a top tennis star during the 1930s and 1940s. He got involved in the sport at age ten while working as a ball boy at the Town Club in his native Milwaukee. He showed a natural talent for the game and developed into a top young player, winning the National Boys and Junior Championships.

An intelligent player with outstanding groundstrokes, Parker won back-to-back U.S. singles titles in 1944 and 1945 while a sergeant in the U.S. Army. Other victories include two French Championships, two Canadian Open Championships, and five U.S. Clay Court Championships. Parker won the 1943 National Doubles with Jack Kramer, the 1948 U.S. National Doubles with Frederick Schroeder, and the 1949 Wimbledon Doubles and French Open Doubles with Pancho Gonzales. His seventeen straight years (1933-49) in the U.S. Top Ten stood as a men's record for nearly forty years, and he was the top ranked player in the world in 1948.

Polish wrestler Wladyslaw Talun portrayed Goliath in a 1950 version of "David and Bathsheba."

After his retirement, he served as an assistant special effects director for the Metro Goldwyn Mayer Studios, and later became sports director for the McClurg Sports Center in Chicago.

*　　*　　*

Wrestling, at least on the professional level, has long been considered to be more spectacle than sport. Still, wrestlers have been among the most visible athletes in America. One of the most famous athletes of the early twentieth century was Stanislaw Cyganiewicz, who wrestled as Zbyszko. A native of Poland, he became a legendary international figure in the 1920s and wrestled until he was sixty. Walter "Killer" Kowalski ranked with "Gorgeous George" as one of the most popular wrestlers of the fifties and sixties. Wladyslaw "Iron" Talun was a muscular 6-8, 300-pound giant who played Goliath in the 1951 film *David and Bathsheba*. Talun could have pursued an acting career in Hollywood, but preferred to wrestle and stay close to his home in Buffalo.

There have been some outstanding Polish American ama-

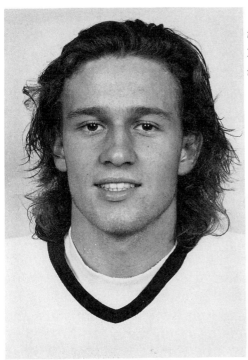

Mariusz Czerkawski joined the Boston Bruins of the NHL in 1994 after playing in the Swedish professional hockey league.

teur wrestlers, including freestyle standout Stan Dziedzic and Greco-Roman wrestlers Dennis and Duane Koslowski.

*   *   *

Polish kids growing up in America and especially Canada, dreamed of becoming hockey stars. Many succeeded, with names like Walter "Turk" Broda, Ed Krzyzanowski, Ed Slowinski, Pete Stempkowski, Jerry Korab, Jim Peplinski, Bob Kudelski, Pat Jablonski and Ed Olczyk among them. Len Ceglarski retired from Boston College as college hockey's all-time winning coach.

Peter Sidorkiewicz, who was born in Darown Bialstocka, Poland and came to Canada at a young age, was a top NHL goalie. Mariusz Czerkawski, a Pole playing professionally in Sweden, joined the NHL Boston Bruins in 1994 and is considered a rising young star.

The man considered hockey's greatest player ever, Wayne Gretzky, often refers to his Polish roots when talking about his amazing success. "The Great One" credits his father, the son of a White Russian father and a Polish mother, for instilling the kind of "old world" values that helped him succeed. Wayne's paternal grandmother, who immigrated from Poland when she was twenty-six-years-old, was also a strong influence. "She never forgot her Polish background," according to Walter Gretzky. She was convinced of young Wayne's future success because, according to a Polish superstition, his hairy arms meant that he would one day become wealthy. She also played hockey with Wayne when he was as young as two, acting as his goalie in the living room of her home.

Wayne developed into a hockey standout at a very young age and became a pro star despite his lack of size and speed. He led the Edmonton Oilers to four NHL championships and became the most recognizable figure in the sport. In 1988 he was traded to the Los Angeles Kings. His move helped increase the popularity of the sport in the United States. He also won nine scoring titles, and in 1981-82 scored an amazing 92 goals. In 1994, Gretzky became the greatest goal scorer in NHL history, breaking Gordie Howe's thirty-one-year-old record of 801 goals.

*   *   *

Bowling has long been a popular sport for working class Americans, an inexpensive recreation that could be played in any season and combined competition and camraderie. Polish Americans in the Bowling Hall of Fame include: Johnny (Krzyminski) Crimmins, who won the first national All-Star tournament in 1941; Ed Lubanski, who captured the 1958 World Invitational Bowling Tournament and was Bowler of the Year in 1959; and Billy Golembiewski, the American Bowling Congress Masters Champion in 1960 and 1962.

*　　*　　*

Poles who immigrated to the United States following the communist takeover after World War II also had an impact on the American sports scene. One of the most remarkable of them was Henryk deKwiatkowski. His father, a Polish cavalry officer, died during the German invasion in 1939. Henryk was caught by the Russians as he tried to flee and sent to a prison camp. After about two years, he escaped and boarded a ship to England, but it was torpedoed off Sierra Leone. One of just seven survivors, Henryk made his way to England and at age sixteen, joined two of his brothers with the Royal Air Force. After the war, he became an aeronautical engineer and later moved to the United States and formed his own aircraft company, brokering the sale of airplanes. He amassed a huge fortune and started buying horses with it. DeKwiatkowski paid just $160,000 for Conquistador Cielo, the Belmont Stakes and horse of the year winner in 1982. He also won the Belmont in 1986 with Danzig Connection. In 1992, he purchased historic Calumet Farm in Kentucky for $17 million. Today deKwiatkowski is considered one of the country's most successful and respected owners of thoroughbred horses

*　　*　　*

College basketball developed into a major sport in the years before World War II. Bob Kurland was an All-America at Oklahoma A&M and led the Aggies to a pair of NCAA Championships in the 1940s. Other standouts included Chet Jaworski and Stan Modzelewski of Rhode Island State, Paul Nowak of Notre Dame, and Ed Sadowski of Seton Hall. Sadowski was one of the sport's first "big men" at 6-5 and 240-pounds and also starred in the fledging professional leagues. In 1941, he led the Detroit Eagles to victory in the invitational World Tournament. Joe Graboski, Vince Boryla and Tom Gola were stars during the formative years of pro basketball, while more recent top players have included Dave Twardzik, Steve Kuberski, Mitch Kupchak, Kelly Tripucka, Mike Gminski, Larry Krystkowiak, Frank Brickowski, Jim Les and Eric Piatkowski.

One of the leading figures in the sport of basketball today is Mike Krzyzewski, who was raised in a working class Polish American family in Chicago. He played basketball at Weber High School, where Coach Al Ostrowski had to threaten the unselfish guard that he would have to run laps if he did not shoot the ball more. Krzyzewski ended up leading the Catholic League in scoring and earned a scholarship to West Point. He played there under Bobby Knight and after serving in the Army, he rejoined Knight as a graduate assistant coach at Indiana. In 1975, Krzyzewski was named head coach at Army, where he put together a five-year record of 73-59.

He came to Duke in 1980 and had to rebuild a program that had a thin talent base. By the 83-84 season, the Blue Devils put together a 24-10 record and earned a NCAA tournament bid, establishing the school as a basketball power.

In 1991, Duke made its fourth NCAA Tournament Final Four appearance, but suffered a 30-point loss to UNLV in the title game. Krzyzewski and his team were determined to avenge the crushing defeat. The following year, Duke faced UNLV in the semifinals and pulled off a 79-77 upset victory. With a 72-65 win over Kansas in the finals, the Blue Devils captured their first ever national championship.

The following year, Krzyzewski became the first coach since the legendary John Wooden to win consecutive titles. Led by All-Americas Christian Laettner and Bobby Hurley (both of whom have Polish roots), Duke defeated Michigan 71-51 to win a second straight NCAA title. It also marked the fifth consecutive year that Duke had been in the Final Four.

Krzyzewski's teams have been a reflection of their coach playing tough, disciplined—basketball with aggressive team defense. His current squad includes talented youngsters Steve Wojiechowski and Taymon Domzalski.

For all of its success on the basketball court, Duke has continued to maintain tough academic standards, which

Krzyzewski takes very seriously. In 1990, he refused to raise the team's Final Four banner because two of his seniors had not completed their requirements for degrees by the end of the school year. It was the first time that had happened since Coach K took over ten years earlier.

It is significant to note that Mike Krzyzewski is probably the best known and most respected sports figure in Polonia today. Not only is he recognized as one of college basketball's greatest coaches, but he never misses an opportunity to remind people about his roots. His pride in his Polish heritage is matched only by his quick wit. (When asked on national TV what advice he would give Nolan Richardson of Arkansas before facing him in a big game, he replied: "Be kind to Polish people.")

But unlike most previous Polish American sports icons, Krzyzewski made his mark not as an athlete but as a coach. His rise from humble beginnings to the helm of the most respected college basketball program in the nation may inspire other Polish Americans to pursue administrative and coaching positions.

*   *   *

Polish Americans have contributed to and benefitted from a wide range of sports. Randy Stoklos is a top volleyball professional. Andy Banachowski is the long-time coach of the women's volleyball team at UCLA. Chet Jastremski, Matt Cetlinski and Rob Darzynkiewicz have been top swimmers. Don Janicki, John Gregorek, and Bill and Gerald Donakowski were outstanding runners. In addition to Stan Ketchel and Tony Zale, top Polish American boxers have included Teddy Yarosz, Henry Chemel, Eddie "Babe" Risko and Bobby Czyz. Richard (Olszewski) Oles was a member of the 1971 World Championship Fencing Team. Mike Kiedrowski was one of the few riders to win American Motorcyclist Association championships in three classes. In billiards, Frank Taberski was a dominant champion of the sport from the early 1900s through the 1930s, while Steve Mizerak won the U.S. Open

Welterweight taekwondo gold medal winner Arlene Limas was the first U.S. gold medal winner at Seoul summer games.

from 1970 through 1973, the PPA World Open title in 1982 and 1983, and the World Pocket Billiards title in 1983 and 1984. George Szypula was a top gymnast who later coached Michigan State to numerous NCAA and Big Ten titles. Norbert (Szymanski) Schemansky and Stan Stanczyk were record-setting weightlifters. Mr. Americas of the 1940s include Frank (Stepniak) Leight (1942), Steve Stanko (1944) and Alan Stephan (1946). Frank Zane was one of the most successful bodybuilders of the 1970s, winning the coveted Mr. Olympia title three times. Danny Kuchcinski twice won the World Horseshoe Pitching Championship. Mark Gorski won Olympic gold in sprint cycling in 1984. Earl Bascom was a top rodeo cowboy.

*　　*　　*

Not many top Polish athletes have come to America in their primes. One reason was that most of the sports in which they excelled were not as popular—or very financially lucrative—in the United States. However, some top Polish athletes came to the United States for better training facilities and coaching, such as ice skater Gregorz Filipowski and Artur Wojdat, who in 1988 became the first Pole to win an Olympic medal in swimming.

When Poland experienced great political turmoil in the 1970s and 1980s, many top athletes and coaches came to the United States. These Poles, like others of the "Solidarity Generation" who came here at that time, tended to be more educated and sophisticated than the earlier Polish immigrants. Many were skilled in sports that relatively few Americans were adept in, such as pentathlon and kayaking.

Janusz Peciak, who won gold for Poland in the modern pentathlon in 1976, came here to coach the American team. Zenon Babraj and Kris Korzenowski (rowing), Eddie Borysiewicz and Andrzej Bek (cycling), and Paul Podgorski (canoeing and kayaking) were all native Poles who coached American teams in the Olympics. In 1984 Borysiewicz coached the U.S. Olympians to their first cycling medals since 1912, as the team won 4 golds, 3 silvers and 2 bronzes, and Podgorski led the U.S. squad to its first gold medals ever in canoe in 1988.

Some Polish soccer stars came to North America in the 1970s, when the sport was at a peak of popularity in the United States and Polish soccer was producing some great teams. Poland won Olympic gold in 1972 and finished 3rd in the 1974 World Cup. One of the best Polish imports was Kaz Deyna. Deyna came here to play in the North American Soccer League and set a NASL record in 1983 by scoring 5 goals and 4 assists in one game.

*   *   *

Professional soccer did not sustain its popularity in this country. A new version of the sport was created, which was played inside on a much smaller surface and called indoor soccer.

Rudy Pikuzinski is considered one of indoor soccer's all-time leading scorer. His father, Rudy Sr., was himself a soccer standout both in his native Poland and in Buffalo and he wanted his son to continue the tradition. While his friends on Sobieski Street were playing football or basketball, young Rudy usually could be found kicking a soccer ball. He also played on numerous amateur teams, including his fathers White Eagle squad.

In his early teens, Rudy Jr. started playing baseball without his father's knowledge and developed into an all-star short-stop. Rudy Sr. finally heard about it and he rushed to the field, stormed onto the diamond in the middle of a game, and dragged his son to soccer practice.

Soccer enjoyed some success in the United States in the 1970s, but Americans seemed to prefer the fast pace of sports like basketball and football. Soccer was taken indoors and played in arenas. Starting with the hometown Buffalo Stallions of the Major Indoor Soccer League, Rudy Jr. tried the new sport and did quite well. The 5-9, 160-pound forward was not only a well-conditioned and skilled athlete, but he had the determination and toughness to excel in the indoor game.

In 1984, he was joined with the Stallions by brother Randy, who at eighteen was the youngest player in league history. Unlike Rudy, a fiesty and aggressive goal-scorer, Randy was a soft-spoken midfielder and defensive standout.

The Stallions folded and the brothers moved to the National Professional Soccer League, where their success continued. Rudy played in seven All-Star games and helped the Canton Invaders win four NPSL championships. He won the NPSL Most Valuable Player Award three straight years.

When Buffalo was awarded a franchise in the NPSL in 1992, the Pikuzinski brothers returned home. They have not only made the Blizzard a competitive team, but helped Buffalo lead the league in attendance. Rudy Pikuzinski Jr., blessed with his father's dedication, work ethic and love of soccer, has already made his mark as one of the sport's best.

FROM HOCKEY PUCKS TO HORSESHOES

*   *   *

Polonia is a very diverse community, and that diversity is reflected in the wide variety of sports in which Polish Americans have had an impact. Although major sports like baseball and football have obviously played a central role in the individual and collective advancement of Polish Americans, many other sports have had important parts in the community's development.

6

GRASS ROOTS
The Role of Polish American Organizations

Sports had a significant direct impact upon the lives of average Polish Americans as well as those who used it to achieve fame and fortune.

In the early part of the twentieth century, athletics became central to life in Polish American neighborhoods, and a variety of organizations that supported and promoted sports activities were established.

The economic changes that took place following World War I encouraged increased involvement in sports, particularly the increased wages and shorter (five or five-and-a-half day) work week. New technologies also helped, such as the electric lights that replaced inefficient gas lamps and allowed for evening athletic activities in indoor gyms and arenas. Working class Polish Americans flocked to these activities which provided inexpensive recreational and social pursuits.

Polish immigrants wasted little time in creating a variety of organizations after they came to this country, even if they had not participated in organized groups in their homeland. America was often hostile to immigrants, and the Poles found comfort and protection by organizing with their own ethnic group. As early as the 1840s, groups like "The Society of Poles in America" and "The Society of the Third of May" were established by Polish immigrants. Many others followed.

The first and only national Polish American organization

dedicated primarily to physical fitness and recreation was the Polish Falcons. The organization had its roots in Europe, starting with the German *turnverein,* or "turning societies" that were established in 1811 to prepare young Germans to fight foreign aggressors. The Turners organized physical fitness activities around gymnastics and mass coordinated exercises. In 1862 the Czechs formed their own *sokols* for a similar purpose, and other Slavic groups followed suit. Some Poles founded their own such group, called *Sokolstwo Polskie* in Austrian-ruled Poland in 1867. Its purpose was to build healthy bodies while promoting Polish patriotism and nationalism. Poland was partitioned at the time, and it was the hope that the physical fitness regimen would prepare young people to one day help Poland regain its independence and rebuild a free and independent nation.

Polish immigrants to the United States brought this concept along with them, and the first Falcons lodge, or nest, in the United States was established in Chicago on June 12, 1887. It was organized by Felix Pietrowicz, a twenty-four-year-old immigrant from Poznan.

By 1894 there were twelve Falcons nests, and four of them formed a federation chartered by the state of Illinois as "Alliance of Polish Turners of the United States of America." The organization dedicated itself to utilizing physical education and sports to develop healthy and patriotic young people.

The Falcons adopted the ancient Latin maxim of "Mens sana in corpore sana." It translated as "w zdrowym ciele zdrowy duch" in Polish and as "a sound mind in a sound body" in English.

In 1914 the organization became "Polish Falcons Alliance of America," and in its purpose statement emphasized the need to prepare to help Poland attain independence. After World War I began, thousands of young men who had undergone paramilitary training with the Falcons volunteered to fight in Europe.

When the war ended and Poland was restored as a nation, the organization put more emphasis on physical fitness activi-

The years between the world wars, Polish American communities rallied behind their sports teams. Here a baseball team sponsored by the Polish National Alliance in Buffalo poses with supporters in front of the Dom Polski (Polish Home).

ties, especially gymnastics—parallel bars, the side horse, the horizontal bars, vaulting horse—and massed coordinated calisthenics and marching drills. In the years that followed, the Falcons continued to add new sports to suit the interests of its members. When the modern Olympic movement began in 1896, track and field events like high jump and shot put were incorporated into the program. After the turn of the century, increasingly popular sports like baseball and cycling were added.

In the 1920s, the official name of the Falcons became "Polish Falcons of America," and the organization also began providing fraternal insurance benefits to its members. This new development did not usurp the existing physical education activities, but helped add to the Falcons financial viability.

Large numbers of Polish Americans were not drawn to the Young Mens Christian Associations which promoted physical fitness throughout America. The YMCAs proclaimed the doctrine of "muscular Christianity," similar in purpose to groups like the Falcons but with a Protestant religious orientation, rather than a nationalist Polish philosophy.

The Falcons' program became very popular before long, and nests were established in virtually every area where there was a significant Polish population. The various Falcons' nests would organize various ongoing sports and recreational activities depending on the interests of its members, and then meet to hold regional and national competitions. Every two years, various districts hold regional competitions, or *zlots*. Every four years, a national zlot was held in conjunction with the national convention. In 1936, the Falcons organized a Polish American Olympics in Pittsburgh, but World War II disrupted plans to make it a regular event.

The Falcons was at its zenith in the 1920s and 1930s with thousands of active participants, including many outstanding athletes, like Stan Musial and Stella Walsh, who participated in their programs.

In the 1930s, young Polish Americans became interested in more American sports such as basketball and bowling, and the Falcons added them to their program. Later golf, volleyball and softball became popular. Like bowling, they were sports that allowed older members to remain physically active. Newer Polish immigrants brought an enthusiasm for soccer to the Falcons, and many nests incorporated that sport into their activities.

A number of other Polish American organizations have played an important part in promoting and sponsoring sports activities of various kinds, both on the national and divisional levels. They include the Polish National Alliance, the Polish Roman Catholic Union of America, the Polish National Union of America, the Alliance of Poles in America and the Union of Poles in America.

But there were organized sports clubs in every Polish

American neighborhood. Most of the time, athletic clubs developed around a neighborhood or parish, often through a church Catholic Youth Organization (CYO). These clubs were where many young people learned the basic sports skills, as well as taught important lessons about discipline and teamwork. They provided healthy activities for young people who usually could not afford what few activities were available at that time. If immigrant parents could not quite understand their childrens growing preoccupation with athletics, they were pleased that the youngsters found an outlet for their passion and energy.

Basketball was one of the favorite sports. It was an inexpensive and accessible activity that was an important part of the fabric of community life in Polish American neighborhoods in the years between the wars. Teams would meet at a local gymnasium, and spectactors would cheer on their friends and neighbors. When the competition was over, the gym was converted into a dance hall and players and spectators would enjoy an evening of socialization.

There were also clubs that were organized around a specific sport, rather than a particular neighborhood. That was frequently the case when Polish immigrants found that most second- and third-generation Polish Americans did not share their enthusiasm for European sports, like soccer. It is believed that the first Polish American soccer club was established in 1923, and was known as Chicago Polonia (later as Chicago Wisla). The club was led by Jan Galazkiewicz, and sponsored by the Polish National Alliance. Similar clubs were established in Polish communities throughout the country,

Polish American community life was altered dramatically by World War II. Not only did the men go to war and undergo a vast array of new experiences, but many of the women who stayed behind moved into industrial jobs for the first time during the wartime labor shortage. At the same time, the post-war economic boom created never before seen opportunities for economic mobility for the working class. The GI bill subsidized higher education for veterans, making college

Thousands gather for opening ceremonies in Buffalo's Civic Stadium for the Polish Falcons' 21st annual Zlot (Athletic Meet) in July 1956.

more accessible than ever.

Polish Americans as a group became more prosperous in the years following the war. Like many Americans, large numbers left the crowded urban ethnic neighborhoods for suburbia. The suburbanization of America, combined with the advent of television and other factors, accelerated the assimilation of Polonia and the decline of many old ethnic institutions. Some survived in some form, like the Falcons, by adjusting to the changes that were taking place in America. In most cases, particularly for the neighborhood groups, they were replaced by non-ethnic organizations like Little League Baseball and Pop Warner Football. In the years following World War II, the sports programs of Polish American groups declined as Polish Americans became more assimilated and joined other non-Polish athletic clubs. As many Polish Americans lost their knowledge of the Polish language and forgot many of the traditions and customs, they felt less of an attraction to these groups. Yet many Polish American organizations, particularly those that were flexible enough to address the needs of the new immigrants, as well as the second, third, and fourth generation Polish Americans, were able to survive and thrive.

The Polish Falcons has been able to prosper through all the changes that have taken place in Polonia. Although still committed to its physical fitness programs, the Falcons now focus more of its attention on its fraternal insurance program. There are some 30,000 members in about 150 nests, about 2,000 of whom are active in the athletic programs on a regular basis. This contrasts to the 1930s, when an estimated 10,000 Falcons were active participants in some type of athletics. "We have tried to change to meet the needs of our members," pointed out current Falcons' President Lawrence Wujcikowski. Recent developments include more advanced training programs for Falcons instructors, and sports and dance programs for "tiny tots" starting at five years old.

Russell Duszak, former sports director of the Polish Roman Catholic Union of America, added that athletic activities organized by other Polish American fraternals are still viable. The PRCUA presently organizes annual bowling, golf, baseball and softball tournaments throughout the east and midwest. The bowling tournaments were particularly popular, attracting as many as 90 teams from around the country. "People from around the country were able to get together year after year and renew friendships," he said. "It was a great combination of sports, heritage, and camaraderie."

*   *   *

In recent years a number of new Polish American sports organizations have been established to promote both sports and cultural activities. They do not serve to provide comfort to Polish Americans and help them gain entry into mainstream

At the 1980 induction of the Polish American Sports Hall of Fame baseball star Bill "Moose" Skowron (left) receives his medallion from Hall founder Ed Browalski, and football standout Zygmunt "Ziggy"Czarobski has his medallion presented by Hall Chairman Dick Gamalski.

America; instead, these organizations encourage an appreciation of Polish heritage and the development of bonds between Poland and Polonia.

In 1972 the, *Polish American Sports Hall of Fame* was created to recognize and honor professional and amateur athletes of Polish descent. Ed Browalski, long-time editor of Detroit's *Polish Daily News*, was the driving force behind its creation and its first chairman. The idea evolved from the annual "Polish Night" celebration that was held at Detroit's Tiger Stadium.

Candidates for the hall are nominated by the Board of Directors of the Hall of Fame, but are elected by the Hall's Sports Council Panel, which is comprised of over 200 members from across the country. Over the years, panel members have included a variety of Polish and non-Polish sports figures, including Dave Anderson of the *New York Times*, Fred Hickman of *CNN Sports* and Dick Vitale of *ESPN*.

The Hall is currently located on the campus of St. Mary's College in Orchard Lake, Michigan, just outside of Detroit. The museum occupies much of the second floor of the Dombrowski Fieldhouse and includes memorabilia donated by its inductees, such as Stella Walsh's track shoes and Tom Gola's basketball jersey.

From its modest beginnings, the hall's annual banquet has grown into a gala affair that draws a capacity crowd of 500 guests. While some have advocated moving the banquet to larger facilities to accomodate the demand, the board has kept it in Detroits Polish Century Club. The dinner maintains a strong ethnic Polish flavor, including the singing of the Polish national anthem, a strolling accordionist, and a menu that includes *golabki, kielbasa*, and other traditional Polish favorites. An annual golf outing is also held to raise funds for the hall.

As part of the festivities, the hall also presents special recognition awards honoring Polish Americans who have advanced in amateur sports. The honorees, mostly from the state of Michigan, includes such local legends as Detroit's Mike Sitkowski and Dorothy Kukulka of Flint.

The board members, mostly from the Detroit area, represent a diverse cross-section of business and government. Many have extensive sports backgrounds, though relatively few have close ties to other Polish American organizations.

In 1993, the board honored Stan Musial at a special reception marking the 20th anniversary of his induction. At that time, Musial announced the creation of a special scholarship fund for students of Polish heritage attending St. Mary's College. "Stan the Man" seeded the fund with a contribution of $11,000, which was matched by the Hall of Fame.

The Polish American Sports Hall of Fame has risen from its modest beginnings to a position of national prominence. Although it has a decidedly Michigan flavor, its membership roster (currently numbering sixty-five) includes most of the top names in Polonia sports, from Danny Abramowicz to Tony Zale.

The *Polish American Sports Foundation* was organized by Alex Kuryllo, a California developer and native of Poland. The group raises funds to bring Polish swimmers to the training facility at Mission Viejo. The first group of eighteen Poles came in 1985 and included Artur Wojdat, who earned a scholarship to the University of Iowa and won Olympic bronze in the 400-meter freestyle in Seoul in 1988. In 1995, Beata Kaszuba of Arizona, another Polish swimmer sponsored by the Foundation, set a world record in the 100-yard breaststroke.

The *Polish American Sport and Cultural Organization* (PASCO) was formed by Stanley Jablonski and Robert Avery, two school teachers from Massachusetts. The non-profit group's expressed goal is to promote understanding between the people of the United States and Poland through sports and cultural activities. PASCO's main project was a summer camp in Poland that brought together teenagers from both countries.

The *Polish National Youth Baseball Foundation* and the *Polish Little League Foundation* are among the organizations created to support baseball by raising funds and collecting equipment for youth baseball in Poland.

* * *

While Polish Americans celebrate the accomplishments of the sports greats who have emerged from Polonia, there are countless individuals involved in grassroots organizations who made a real and substantial impact in their communities. By organizing, coaching and sponsoring sports activities on the local level, they were able to have a direct positive impact on the lives of many Polish Americans.

In 1984, David Franczyk profiled three of Buffalo's "flesh and blood legends" in the *Polish American Voice*. He wrote of the many contributions of Peter Machnica, Dan "Peanuts" Zackiewicz, and Peter Raczynski, three local sports organizers and coaches:

After hitting the 'big time, the sports 'superstars of Polish descent may come back to the old neighborhood, but it can never be the same, and unfortunately sometimes the only legacy they leave behind is their own high batting average or pass completions. Did these people really touch our lives? No, often it seems that the real sports superstars aren't those who make the major leagues, but those real-life heroes who dedicated their lives to sport and their local community.

There have been countless of these "unsung heroes" across Polonia. Their names may not be nationally known, but their contributions have been immeasurable. Every Polish American community has at least one—probably more—dedicated individual who has devoted much time and effort to teaching and coaching young people. Casey Plewacki in Cleveland, Tony Lutomski in Detroit, and Joe Osmanski in Chicago are just a few of those who improved the lives of others through sports.

7

GREAT STRIDES
Polish American Women in Sports

As modern sports took shape in America in the nineteenth century, women were excluded from many of the activities. An ideal of "true womanhood," imported from Victorian England, depicted women as delicate and passive, unable to withstand strenuous exercise. It was not until late in the century when many doctors started recommending that women engage in exercise to promote their health, albeit in moderation. More women, usually those from the leisure classes, became involved in athletic pursuits, usually tennis, archery, fencing, and golf.

A major factor that limited women's sports participation was clothing. The hooped skirts and other restrictive dress of the time made it very difficult for women to have the free movement necessary to properly perform many sports. The emergence of the bicycle as a popular form of transportation and recreation helped change the exisiting mores, since it required women to abandon ankle-length dresses for bloomers or split skirts. Those changes in clothing accelerated womens participation in sports.

Despite the widespread perception of women as "the weaker sex," Polish American and other ethnic women often worked alongside men in the fields and factories. But like their male counterparts, it was difficult for working class Polish American women to find the time to participate in sports a great deal.

The postwar economic boom created new opportunities for poor and working-class women to participate in leisure activities. Social changes (such as women receiving the right to vote) prompted women to seek access to male-dominated arenas. Still, it was a very slow process for women to gain full acceptance into many sports. There was limited acceptance of women in some sports such as tennis, though women's tennis matches were reduced to best-of-three sets (rather than best-of-five). Women who played sports like baseball and basketball were openly ridiculed by many. The International Olympic Committee allowed women to compete in golf and tennis in the second Olympiad in Paris in 1900, but only slowly allowed expansion into other sports. (No track events were added until 1928; women's basketball was included for the first time in 1976).

Women members of the Polish Falcons were given a relatively high degree of participation in the organization. Women were encouraged to take part in the physical fitness activities, and could organize their own groups associated with the men's nests, though they did not have equal status with the men. In 1897, Stefania Chmielinska, the Falcons first female instructor, and Teofila Samolinska appealed to the Falcons board for "full, not half equality" for women in the organization. Citing the organizations possible involvement in future military campaigns, the directors declined. The women then established the Polish Womens Alliance, which did not have the same emphasis on athletics as the Falcons. The Polish Falcons continued to attract many women who wanted to participate in sports.

*   *   *

Despite much outright hostilty and the efforts to restrict women's involvement, many women sought to participate in sports that were considered "masculine." One of the pioneering women's sports teams was the Philadelphia Bobbies, the first all-female professional baseball team.

Loretta (Jaszczak) Jester was one of the charter members of the Bobbies. She grew up on a farm northeast of Philadelphia and played all kinds of sports with the local boys. In 1924, when she was sixteen, Loretta responded to a newspaper ad seeking female baseball players. She made the squad and became a member of the Bobbies power hitting quartet known as "The Four Horsemen." The team played against male and female competition and toured Japan. "Sticks" Jester later married Walter Lipski and raised a family. Later, she admitted that she no longer had much interest in the sport, saying: "In my day, people played because they loved the game and didn't worry about what they could get out of it."

*　　*　　*

One of the greatest female athletes of all time was Stanislawa Walasiewicz, better known as Stella Walsh. She was born in Poland in 1911 and came to the United States with her parents when she was two. She began running at an early age and in 1930, became the first woman to break the 11-second barrier for the 100-yard dash.

In 1930 Walsh set her first of many world records, competing in the 50-yard dash at Madison Square Garden. She emerged as a favorite to win gold in the sprints in the 1932 Los Angeles Olympics.

As the Olympics approached, Stella lost her position with the New York Central Railroad, due to financial cutbacks resulting from the world-wide depression. It was difficult for her to find work, but she was eventually offered a job with the Cleveland Recreation Department. However, she was told that accepting the job would make her ineligible to compete in the Olympics. The rules disqualified athletes who earned a living from any kind of sports or recreational activities.

Stella did receive one other job offer. The Polish consulate in New York City offered her a position, which was predicated on her maintaining her Polish citizenship. After agonizing over the decision at length, a day before she was to receive her United States naturalization papers, Stella chose to work for the Polish consulate.

Competing for Poland in the 1932 Olympics, Walsh lived up to all expectations. She won the 100-meter run in a world record-tying time of 11.9 seconds, after having tied the world mark in both of her preliminary heats. She also finished 6th in the discus, with a throw of 110 feet, 3 inches.

She was criticized by some Americans for competing for Poland, while others pointed out that her case epitomized the inadequate support in this country for amateur athletics, particularly women's athletics.

Stella continued to compete and was virtually unbeatable in the early 1930s. She set hundreds of records, including world records for the 100, 200, 60 and 70. She ran for Poland again in the 1936 Berlin Olympics and improved her 100-meter time to 11.7, but finished second to American Helen Stephens.

In 1947, after becoming a U.S. citizen, Walsh hoped to compete for the American Olympic team. Olympic officals rejected her effort because she had previously competed for Poland. In 1956 she married Harry Olson, a draftsman from California, and again asked for a spot on the U.S. team. Since she was married to an American, Walsh was offered a chance to join the American team, but failed to qualify. She was forty-five years old.

Stella remained active in sports, both as a coach and as a newspaper writer. She later worked for the Cleveland Recreation Department, organizing various womens sports and recreational programs. She was also active with the Polish Falcons and other Polish American organizations.

In 1980 Walsh went to a discount store in Cleveland to buy some decorations for a reception for the Polish National Womens Basketball team, which was about to play at Kent State. Walsh apparently walked into a robbery attempt and was found shot to death in the store's parking lot.

A huge controversy erupted when an autopsy revealed that Walsh had a condition known as mosaicism, a rare condition which involves ambiguous sexual organs. There were even reports that Walsh was really a man.

In his report, Cuyahoga County Coroner, Samuel R. Gerber, concluded that Walsh "lived and died a female." He stated that Walsh had non-functional male sex organs, but both male and female chromosomes. Gerber added that, had Walsh been born thirty years later, medical science likely would have quickly ended any ambiguity about her gender. Shortly after her birth, "a decision would have been made as to whether the child should be raised as a male or female....then reconstructive surgery would be performed." When the surgery was completed, "this child would appear and lead the life of an individual of the chosen sex."

Gender is determined by five variables: chromosomes, hormones, gonads, external genitalia and gender assignment, or what gender the person is raised as. Most people fall into one of two categories, male and female, but not all.

In the late 1960s, when women began breaking records, organizers of international amateur competitions began giving "gender tests" to women athletes. The tests did not turn up any men masquerading as women, but rather a number of various genetic anomalies. Questions about the effectiveness of the tests, as well as their real relevance, led the International Amateur Athletic Federation to recommend abolishing all gender verification testing.

A misunderstanding of her condition led some of her former rivals to try to have Walsh posthumously stripped of her titles. However, there was no evidence that Walsh's genetic anomaly gave her any athletic advantage over her competitors. "Most of the girl athletes thought she wasn't exactly kosher," said one-time rival Helen Stephens, "but it was an unfortunate case of birth defects."

The fact is that very few athletes, male or female, have had careers that could be compared to Stella Walsh. She was extraordinarily versatile, setting women's world records in all of the sprint events. She was a top discus thrower and long jumper and won numerous pentathlon championships. Walsh was also an outstanding basketball and softball player. Her track career was one of the longest of any athlete, as she competed for more than twenty years. She won three Amateur Athletic Union championships at age thirty-seven and the AAU long jump at age forty.

Walsh had a difficult life; when she died she was making $10,400 a year from her position with the Cleveland Recreation Department, the highest salary that she had ever earned. Despite the controversy that surrounded her death, Walsh is remembered fondly by many, particularly the Polish American community. "She was a fantastic athlete and a fantastic person," recalled Edmund Pett, long-time National Youth Director for the Falcons.

*　　*　　*

The social and economic changes brought about by World War II helped major league baseball lose much of its top talent to the war effort. At the same time, American women were gravitating to jobs and professions that had been dominated by men, and womens sports were steadily increasing in popularity. The result was the creation of the first womens professional sports league in 1943: the All American Girls Baseball League. The top female baseball and softball players in the country were recruited to play, including Jenny Romatowski, Helen Filarski, Alice Blaski, Jean Malanowski, and Sylvia Wronski.

One of the best was Connie Wisniewski, who was named the AAGBL Player of the Year in 1945. Pitching for the Rapid City Chicks, she posted a remarkable 32-11 record and a 0.81 ERA that season. She also became known as "The Iron Woman" for her remarkable stamina and endurance. While her male counterparts were pitching once every four or five days, on three occasions Connie pitched both games of a doubleheader—and twice she won both games. That season

Stella Walsh crosses the finish line ahead of Constance Darnowski in a heat of the 60-meter dash at the 1950 National AAU Senior Pentathlon Championship for Women. The 39-year-old Walsh won the pentathlon with 1,929 points for the 5 events. Darnowski finished 5th in the pentathlon.

she pitched to 1,367 batters in 391 innings.

Connie was spotted by a scout while playing softball in Detroit and asked her mothers permission to join the fledgling league. Mrs. Wisniewski was reluctant about letting her daughter play professional baseball, but when Connie started talking about joining the service instead, her mother relented.

Wisniewski began her career in 1944 with the Chicks, who were then in Milwaukee. Despite a knee injury, she posted a 23-10 record. After her remarkable season in 1945, she had an even better year in 1946, turning in a 33-9 record for a .786 won-loss percentage. She lost the Player of the Year Award to Sophie Kurys, who had stolen 201 bases in 203 attempts that year. Connie was named the All-Star pitcher, however.

The AAGPBL began by playing what was basically softball, but the rules gradually changed to be more like baseball. Wisniewski was an underhand pitcher, but in 1948 the league required pitchers to throw overhand. Connie was unable to make the adjustment and thought she would have to leave the game. Her manager suggested she switch to the outfield, and she agreed. Connie immediately became an All-Star at that position, hitting .289 (third best in the league) with 7 home runs and 20 doubles.

In 1950, Connie jumped to the Chicago National Girls Baseball League, a fast-pitch softball league that offered to increase her salary from $100 to $250 a week. When the Chicks agreed to match her salary, she returned to the AAGBL the following year. In 1952, when she turned thirty, Wisniewski decided to retire and take a job at General Motors. Over her career, the five-time All-Star had posted a 107-48 pitching record and a .275 batting average.

In 1954, a variety of social and economic factors led to the the demise of the once hugely popular league. It was an obscure footnote in sports history until *A League of Their Own*, a movie based on the league, was released to critical and popular acclaim. It was not until almost forty years after the demise of the AAGBL that a womens professional baseball team, the Colorado Silver Bullets, managed by Phil Niekro, played against mens semipro teams.

*   *   *

No one in the history of sports has ever had a more fitting nickname than Carol "Blaze" Blazejowski. Her extraordinary athletic talent, relentless determination, and uncompromising work ethic made Blaze one of the brightest stars in the history of women's basketball and a trailblazer for women's sports in this country.

Blaze is the leading scorer in women's Division I college basketball history, having tallied 3,199 points during her remarkable career at Montclair State College from 1974 to

1978. No other woman has ever surpassed that mark, and just three men (Pete Maravich, Freeman Williams and Lionel Simmons) have ever scored more. Despite subsequent rule changes designed to enhance offensive output, particularly the 3-point shot, some sixteen years after the end of Carol Blazejowski's collegiate career her scoring record remains intact.

But Carol did more than put the ball in the basket. She was a superb, all-around talent, a team-oriented player skilled in all facets of the game. Her awards and achievements were many, including collegiate women's basketball player of the year honors, first team All-America selection for three straight seasons, captaincy of the U.S. Women's Olympic Basketball Team, and the Most Valuable Player honors and the scoring title in the women's professional league. In 1994, she was inducted into the National Basketball Hall of Fame in Springfield, Massachusetts.

Carol grew up in Cranford, New Jersey, a township of about 24,000 people. As a youngster, she spent much of her spare time in pick-up basketball games, playing—and usually out-playing—the boys. Her parents "didn't think there was anything wrong with their little girl wanting to play with the boys, as long as I came home and said that I beat them." A tremendous natural athlete, Carol was also an outstanding softball pitcher and shortstop.

As a senior, Carol led Cranford High School's first varsity girls' basketball team to 19 straight wins and a berth in the state finals. Blaze averaged 31.4 points and 17 rebounds a game and earned All-State recognition. She was a great natural talent and an intense competitor, but also an intelligent player who valued teamwork.

Not surprisingly, Carol became known as "The Blaze." She once asked her father why he did not shorten his last name. Her father responded prophetically, "Blaze isn't my name—someday you'll be proud of that name."

Carol moved on to Montclair State College in New Jersey in 1974, a time when no women received athletic scholarships.

As a freshman, she averaged "just" 19.9 points a game, hitting 43 percent of her shots from the field. As a sophomore, she averaged 28.5 points and earned her first of three straight All-America selections. She improved her scoring average to 34 points a game as a junior, and then to 38.8 as a senior, and led the nation in scoring both years. After her freshman season, she never shot less than 55 percent from the field.

On March 6, 1978, Blaze helped womens college basketball come of age. In New York's Madison Square Garden, Montclair State played Queens College before 12,336 fans. Despite being in foul trouble, Blaze played the entire second half and made an incredible 17 of 21 field goal attempts. She finished with 52 points, a single-game collegiate scoring record for that venue which still stands. Montclair State won the game, 102-91, and women's college basketball was propelled into the national spotlight.

Later that year, Blaze led Montclair State to the AIAW Final Four. Despite Carol's 40 points, Montclair State lost in the semi-finals to eventual champion UCLA.

When Carol ended her collegiate career in 1978, she had scored 3,199 points for an average of 31.7 points per game. Both were Women's Division I College Basketball records. In her senior year, she also set the women's single season record of 1,235 points (38.6 ppg). Over her career, she shot an amazing 54 percent from the field and 79 percent from the free throw line. Blaze also averaged 10.4 rebounds a game.

Carol picked up a variety of honors during her amazing career. She was a three-time All-America selection (1976, 1977 and 1978), was named the Converse Women's Player of the Year Award in 1977, and was the first-ever recipient of the Wade Trophy as women's basketball player of the year in 1978.

The rise in popularity of women's basketball led to the creation of the Women's Basketball League in 1978, but Carol decided to instead pursue her dream of winning Olympic gold. After college, she played in various international competitions, helping U.S. squads win gold medals in the World University Games, the World Championships, and the R.

William Jones Cup in 1979. When tryouts were held for the 1980 team, Carol not only made the squad, but was named captain as well. Unfortunately, the United States decided to boycott the Moscow Games, and Carol's dream to play in the Olympics remained unfulfilled.

Blaze then turned pro with the New Jersey franchise in the WBL for the 1980-81 season and led the Gems into the playoffs for the first time. She was the circuit's top scorer with 1,067 points (29.6 ppg), an All-Star and was named league MVP. The financially troubled WBL folded shortly afterwards and Carol moved on to other endeavors.

Carol eventually joined the National Basketball Association as a licensing director in the NBA's licensing division. She still plays pick-up basketball, but now tries to "channel my competitiveness and passion into my work."

Carol Blazejowski never received an athletic scholarship, but such scholarships now exist for women as a direct result of Title IX. Enacted into law in 1972, Title IX of the Educational Amendment Act provided a major boost to womens athletics on the scholastic level by banning gender discrimination at institutions receiving federal funding. Nevertheless, womens sports remained secondary to mens sports, especially in regard to leadership positions and professional sports opportunities.

Over the years, some Polish American women who have been important figures on the womens sports scene are ice skaters Janet Lynn (Nowicki) and Elaine Zayak, gymnast Ruth Grulkowski, college basketball standouts Mary "Mo" Ostrowski and Susan Rojcewicz, bowlers Ann Setlock and Aleta (Rzepecki) Sill, Candlepin Bowling record-setter Stasia (Milas) Czernicki, and track stars Frances (Sobczak) Kaszubski and Wanda Wejzgrowicz. These women helped destory the myths about women in sports and have created new opportunities for today's generation.

Today, Polish American women continue to participate in and contribute to sports, and enjoy the various benefits of athletics. Athletes like basketball standouts Tracy Lis and

Michelle Marciniak, golfer Betsy (mother's maiden name: Szymkowicz) King, martial arts standout Arlene Limas, and ice skaters Calla Urbanski, Tonia Kwiatkowski and Tara Lipinski are among them. They are continuing the effort to gain full recognition for womens athletics, as well as achieving better performances and leadership positions within their fields.

8

OPENING DOORS
The Opportunities of Sports

"**W**ithout football, where would I be?" Lou Michaels openly wondered during his 1994 induction into the Polish American Sports Hall of Fame. In a broader sense, Polish Americans could ask "Without sports, where would we be?"

Sports helped provide economic mobility for Polish Americans other than athletes, coaches and administrators. For many, sports provided opportunities and experiences that enabled them to pursue and excel in other interests and professions.

*   *   *

Bob Kurland was able to combine basketball and business at the same time. Basketball's first 7-foot star and two-time consensus All-America, he led Oklahoma A&M to NCAA titles in 1945 and 1946 and was named Most Valuable Player in both tournaments.

The great-grandson of Polish immigrants grew to 6-feet-6-inches tall by the time he was thirteen years old. Despite some coordination problems due to his rapid growth, he worked hard to develop into a standout high school basketball player and high jumper. In 1943, the St. Louis, Missouri, native enrolled at Oklahoma A&M, where he played under the legendary Hank Iba. By the time he was a sophomore, he was 7-feet tall and the team's starting center, averaging 17 points a game. He became so adept at batting shots from the rim of the basketball that the practice—known as goaltending—was made illegal by the NCAA. Instead of hurting Kurland, the rule change helped him develop more all-around skills.

Bob led the Aggies to the NCAA championship as a junior, scoring a tournament record of 65 points in three games. The following season, Kurland scored an NCAA record 643 points, and Oklahoma A&M again won the NCAA title.

After graduating in 1947 with a degree in engineering, Kurland rejected offers of as much as $15,000 to play professional basketball. Because of his "conservative nature," he preferred more stability and security than the formative pro basketball league could offer. Kurland opted to enroll in the executive training program for former collegiate athletes that was offered by Phillips Petroleum. Bob played basketball for the Phillips 66ers squad, which competed in the Amateur Athletic Union basketball team and was considered on a par with the pro leagues at that time. In six years, his team posted a 369-26 record and won three AAU titles. Since he maintained his amateur status, Kurland was able to play on the gold medal-winning U.S. basketball teams in the 1948 and 1952 Olympics.

When the 1955 AAU season ended, Bob retired and became a full-time executive with Phillips and later managed special product sales in the marketing division.

*　　*　　*

Tom Gola was an outstanding basketball player in Philadelphia who led his CYO team and his LaSalle High School team to citywide championships. He went on to star for LaSalle College in Philadelphia, leading the Explorers to NIT and NCAA championships in the 1950s.

The 6-foot-6-inch Gola was drafted by his hometown Philadelphia Warriors. The team already had a potent tandem of forwards (Joe Graboski and Paul Arizin), so Tom switched to the backcourt, becoming one of pro basketball's first big

An All-Conference guard and assistant coach for the Wake Forest men's basketball team in the 1960's, Billy Packer (Paczkowski) is an Emmy Award winning basketball analyst for CBS-TV Sports.

guards. The Warriors won the NBA title in 1956. After his retirement, he was elected to the Basketball Hall of Fame.

As a Philadelphia native who spent most of his illustrious playing career in "The City of Brotherly Love," Gola was a prominent person in his home town. He decided to run for the Pennsylvania Legislature and, even though he ran as a Republican in a largely Democratic area, was successful. He was also elected Comptroller of Philadelphia in 1970 and later left politics to pursue a successful business career.

*   *   *

Another sports legend in Philadelphia was Ron Jaworski, the talented quarterback who was known as "The Polish Rifle." Jaworski realized at an early age that he did not want to follow his father into the steel mills of Lackawanna, New York. He played college football at Youngstown State and was drafted by the Los Angeles Rams. It was not until Jaworski was traded to Philadelphia that he blossomed as a pro. He emerged as one of the top passers in the league and helped turn the Eagles into a contender. In 1980, he was NFC Player of the Year and led the Eagles to their only Super Bowl appearance. He ended his career in 1989 with Kansas City, with 2,127 completions and 179 touchdown passes to his credit.

Ron returned to the Philadelphia area and continued the business career he began during his playing days. He owns a number of golf courses and country clubs in the region and is a regular football commentator on ESPN.

*   *   *

A record-setting college basketball career helped propel Henry Nowak, the son of a radiator factory worker from Warsaw, to the U.S. Congress.

Hank enjoyed sports while growing up in Buffalo's largely Polish Black Rock neighborhood, but was cut the first time he tried out for the Riverside High School basketball team. He grew a few inches and came back as a junior to not only make the squad but to also become team captain. He developed into one of the top players in the city and won a scholarship to Canisius College. "College was very important to my mother," he recalled. "Basketball was very important to my father."

Playing from 1954 to 1957, Nowak scored a school-record 1,449 points and led the Golden Griffins to the NCAA quarterfinals for three consecutive years. He passed up an offer to play for the St. Louis Hawks so that he could attend law school.

In 1965, the county Democratic Party was looking for someone to make a "sacrificial run" against the long-time County Comptroller. The reserved Nowak was not a slick politician, but the name he made for himself playing basketball helped the young attorney pull off a major upset. In 1974, he made a successful run for Congress and was re-elected eight times before retiring. In Washington, Nowak was known as a quiet but effective representative who brought millions of dollars of public works projects to Buffalo.

*   *   *

Ed Rutkowski was a native of Kingston, Pennsylvania, who earned a football scholarship to the University of Notre Dame. After leaving the Fighting Irish, he played for the Buffalo Bills from 1963 to 1968. He was not an All-pro player but was a solid receiver who could also return kicks and play several other positions. In 1968, his versatility came to the fore when the Bills lost starting quarterback Jack Kemp and a half-dozen replacements to injury. Finally the team had to turn to Rutkowski, the designated "disaster quarterback." He did not have a great deal of success on the field, but Rutkowski gained the respect and admiration of the community for his noble effort under difficult circumstances. The Bills 1-12-1 record was mitigated somewhat by the fact that by virtue of having the worst record in the league, Buffalo was able to draft the top college player in the country, O.J. Simpson.

Rutkowski went into business and broadcasting before entering politics. For nine years (until 1987) he served as Erie County Executive, the top elective position in the Buffalo area. (He was eventually defeated by a Democratic Assemblyman named Dennis Gorski, an accomplished amateur athlete whose main accomplishment at the time was bringing New York's Olympic-style Empire State Games to Buffalo).

*   *   *

Larry Kaminski grew up in Cleveland, the son of a forge worker and a nurse. He was an All-City football player at Cathedral Latin High School and earned a scholarship to Purdue. Larry was an All-Big Ten center for the Boilermakers in 1966 but was too small to be seriously considered as a pro prospect. Armed with a degree in Industrial Management, he passed up a chance to work for U.S. Steel in order to sign a free agent contract with the Denver Broncos. Despite his lack of size and a variety of injuries, Larry had a solid eight-year career with Denver.

During his off-seasons, Kaminski had worked at various jobs, including one as a merchandising representative for Coors Brewery. When his career was over, he and another former Bronco took over a small beverage distributorship. In a few years, B&K Distributorship grew from a two-person operation into a multi-million dollar business.

*   *   *

Most Polish Americans coming from working-class backgrounds did not gravitate to higher education. Polish families frequently depended on their children to help support them, so a college education was often considered a very costly and unnecessary undertaking. Even if they could afford college, young Polish Americans often did not have the confidence to give up steady employment in factories or mines to pursue a higher education. While the Polish American enclaves gave immigrants and their children a sense of security and comfort, stepping outside the neighborhood boundaries was usually a difficult and traumatic experience. Athletics provided Polish Americans with more than just a way to make a college education affordable; it made them feel more at ease in their new surroundings and helped them attain status and respect in the eyes of their peers.

For women, those opportunities have never been as great, though women like Carol Blazejowski are now using athletics to help themselves advance professionally.

Chet Mutryn credits athletics with giving him personal confidence that allowed him to make the transition from football to business. "Because of sports, I've never been reluctant about approaching strangers and going to strange places," he said. "Sports gave me the self-assurance to try new experiences."

Even if they did not excel in the college-oriented sports like football and basketball, Polish Americans gained much from their sports experience. Their athletic achievements helped them build reputations and status, develop associations, and acquire new insights and understanding.

9

POLISH JOCKS AND POLISH JOKES

Alan Kulwicki created a lot of excitement in the Polish American community when he won his first NASCAR race in 1988. Not only did he capture the Phoenix 500, but he celebrated his win in a distinctive way. Kulwicki drove his car backwards around the track, in what he called his "Polish victory lap." His action was criticized by many in Polonia and he eventually decided to discontinue the practice.

Many Polish Americans were sensitive about the anti-Polish humor that became commonplace in America in the 1960s and early 1970s. The "Polish joke" depicted Polish Americans as an unintelligent and brutish people, and Polish American organizations launched campaigns to promote a more positive image for Polonia. There were many in Polonia who felt that Polish American sports figures did not do enough to counteract this phenomenom, and that their very success in sports contributed to the negative stereotype. After all, athletes have long been stereotyped as "dumb jocks," and Polish Americans have been identified with sports for many years.

Around the turn of the century, Poles were stereotyped as lazy scoundrels. By the 1940s, a new stereotype emerged. Poles were depicted as being tough, unflappable and good-natured, a stereotype that still persists to some extent. It is probably based on some of the high-profile Polish Americans like Stan Musial and Tony Zale, who were model citizens as well as great athletes. Respected and articulate Polish American athletes like Carl Yastrzemski and Phil Niekro became very visible when sports developed into a national obsession in the 1960s. Tony Kubek, the New York Yankee infielder who became a broadcaster on NBC-TVs "Game of the Week," was a dignified and knowledgeable announcer who often referred to his Polish heritage while doing the national telecasts of major league baseball games.

The fact that Polonia became the target of derisive jokes in the 1960s and 1970s likely had much to do with the fact that it is a large, mostly blue-collar community, and probably had much of its basis in latent anti-immigrant and anti-working class sentiment. Polonia's sports achievements certainly made it a more visible target than other more anonymous ethnic communities with similar backgrounds.

While leaders of organized Polonia rallied against the Polish joke, most Polish American sports figures just laughed it off or ignored it. There were a few reasons for that. Athletes, especially those in team sports, tend to use what is called "locker room humor." Basically, it is a very biting form of wit that takes aim at a person's appearance, misfortune, ethnicity—anything is "fair game." It is often used as a form of initiation, to determine if an athlete can withstand verbal abuse. An athlete who "can't take a joke" often loses the respect of his teammates and is usually subjected to even more ridicule.

As Chet Mutryn put it: "It seems to be part of the nature of Polish people to try to get along with others, to fit in." Polish immigrants won acceptance into American industry through their willingness to take the toughest jobs, work long and hard, and not complain. In the same way, Polish American athletes took the abuse that was sometimes heaped upon them without complaint. Just as a boxer might take a punch without flinching to show that his opponent could not hurt him, Polish American athletes refused to show that they were bothered by the sometimes rancorous remarks.

Duke Basketball Coach Mike Krzyzewski has been criticized for telling Polish jokes in public. As Krzyzewski explains it,

Mike Krzyzewski "gets airborne" near the end of NCAA Southeast Regional Championships in Knoxville, March 26, 1994.

it is his intention to let his audience know that he is Polish, while disarming anyone else who might want to tell a Polish joke. For "Coach K," one of the most successful and most respected coaches in college basketball, to tell a Polish joke only serves to remind the listener just how ludicrous the stereotype really is.

Most Polish American athletes seem to feel that, however tasteless Polish jokes may be, most of the time they are essentially harmless. They also tend to have more self-esteem, so they do not feel as threatened by such remarks. As Krzyzewski put it: "If we're so callous that we can't make fun of ourselves, then our race is in pretty sad shape."

In years past, Poles were subjected not just to ridicule but to strong prejudice. As a result, many Polish American athletes were convinced to "Americanize" their names, including Tony (Zaleski) Zale, Al (Szymanski) Simmons, and Frank (Pajkowski) Parker. For many years, ethnics were urged to change their surnames to fit into the "American melting pot."

Many recognized that a Polish surname was a liability in their efforts to succeed in mainstream America. That was true even during the 1860s, when Poles were somewhat exotic and highly respected in America for their heroic uprisings against their oppressors. During the American Civil War, the U.S. Senate twice passed on promotions recommended by President Abraham Lincoln for Polish-born Brigadier General Wlodzimierz Krzyzanowski, despite his exemplary record. The reason, according to Krzyzanowski's commander, was "there was nobody there who could pronounce his name."

Not only did Polish Americans encounter hostility, but most really wanted to fit into American society. Some changed their names to make a break with "the old ways" and become "true Americans." However, most simply saw it as one more accomodation they had to make to survive in America and to make sure that their employment applications were not automatically discarded. They spoke Polish, followed Polish traditions, and lived in a Polish neighborhood, so giving up their Polish name did not seem to really detract from their own ethnicity.

That trend began to fade in the 1930s, as Polish Americans in greater numbers started to resist admonitions to change their names. The success of great athletes who kept their Polish names—such as football greats Alex Wojciechowicz and Ed Danowski—played an important part in convincing Polish Americans to take pride in their names (Wojciechowicz almost shortened his name, but eventually decided that his real name would be more memorable).

Their success in athletics helped the country recognize the many positive contributions of Polish people. Bill Jauss, sports writer for the *Chicago Tribune*, recalled that when Richard "Chico"Kurzawski truned in an inspired performance for the Northwestern football team, legendary coach Woody Hayes told him: "Chico, you are as courageous as the Polish airmen of the R.A.F." Hayes was referring to the Polish pilots who fought with the British Royal Air Force during World War II, and had a reputation for great ability and valor. For many years, the only Polish names that received any national attention were the names of athletes. They not only became special heroes to Polonia, but they became American heroes as well. They were not only tremendous athletes, but many exhibited admirable personal qualities that earned them wide respect. Like the masses of Polish Americans who toiled anonymously to build this nation, for the most part they tended to be "solid citizens" who led quiet, law-abiding lives.

Perhaps the attitude of many Polish American athletes towards the "Polish joke" is revealed in this story told by Mike Krzyzewski. He tells of his days of playing college basketball at West Point for Bobby Knight, who is known for his sharp tongue. Dissatisfied with Krzyzewski's play during a practice session, he berated him as "a dumb Polack." Krzyzewski called his mother that night, telling her about how upset he was over Coach Knight's remarks. Her response was simply: "At least he's talking to you."

10

POLONIA AND SPORTS, TODAY AND TOMORROW

Mike Krzyzewski was saying good-bye to his family at the Raleigh-Durham airport one day when he was approached by an elderly man with tears in his eyes. "He told me that he had been born in Poland and had grown up—like my father—at a time when Polish people faced a lot of prejudice in this country," recalled Krzyzewski. "He said that seeing me succeed was one of the most wonderful things that has ever happened to him, and he loved what I stood for." When the man was finished, both he and Krzyzewski were in tears.

The Polish American community had undergone a great deal of change over the course of this century, but sports continues to be a powerful force. It has helped create unprecedented economic, educational and social opportunities for a community that once had little chance of taking full advantage of the opportunities of America. Young Polish Americans no longer just aspire to be football or baseball players, but they can become doctors, lawyers, even politicians.

America has also changed a great deal, and the close-knit, urban ethnic communities that were once commonplace are now disappearing quickly. Sports has served to accelerate many of those changes by helping break down barriers between communities and promoting assimilation. At the same time, however, it has unified and strengthened Polonia and it continues to do so today.

Mike Krzyzewski is a particularly important sports figure for Polonia today; not only is he very proud of his working-class Polish roots, but his accomplishments are in the higher levels of the sports hierarchy that have had relatively little Polish American representation.

Today, much is written about the "false promise" that sports offers minorities who dream of improving their status through athletic achievement. Many impoverished young people view sports as their salvation, not realizing that only a tiny percentage of them will ever earn a living as an athlete, coach or sports administrator. (Interestingly, basketball is the sport where Polish Americans are well-represented in high-level positions, including general managers Dave Twardzik of Golden State and Mitch Kupchak of the Los Angeles Lakers, broadcaster Billy Packer, and Carol Blazejowski of the NBA.)

Those kinds of unrealistic expectations were not as great a problem for Polish Americans and other ethnics who were trying to gain a toehold in mainstream America during the World War II era. Back then, sports was not as financially lucrative as it is today. Even in the 1950s, all but the highest paid players had to work in the offseason to supplement their incomes. As a result, sports was less considered an ultimate achievement as it was a stepping stone to new opportunities, a way to get a college degree or bankroll a business. Young people of the past were also given more support and guidance because of the more stable home lives, solid neighborhoods, strict schools and strong religious values that existed in the 1940s and 1950s.

Although traditional Polish peasant culture discouraged education and ambition, the lure of sports was strong enough to cause many young Polish Americans to break out of their established patterns of behavior.

There are those who argue that the progress of Polish Americans lags behind that of other comparable ethnic groups, particularly in terms of its representation in upper management positions. While that may be true, Polonia has made some remarkable gains, especially in light of its modest beginnings and the many impediments to its progress. In *Ethnic America*, Thomas Sowell pointed out that in the 1920s, the average IQ of a Polish American was 85, well below the national average of 100. By the 1970s, their IQ level had risen an amazing 24 points to 109. He also cited census figures that showed that Polish Americans exceeded the national family income average index and ranked ahead of the Italian, German and Anglo-Saxon ethnic groups, among others. Obviously Polish Americans have made advancements, and there is much evidence that suggests that sports played a role in those advancements.

If sports today plays a lesser role in determining Polonia's economic and social status, it may be taking on an even greater role in maintaining its viability as an ethnic community. As the use of Polish language and customs declines, the Polish American tradition of sports and athletics has increased value as a unifying force. This is particularly true among younger and more assimilated Polish Americans, who may not observe Polish holiday traditions and probably do not belong to a Polish cultural society. For them, the Polish American tradition of sports could be the strongest link to their ethnic heritage.

Sports has strengthened the bonds between "old Polonia" (descendants of the pre-World War II immigrants) and "new Polonia" (post-World War II emigres and their children). As with most ethnic groups, there are differences between people who arrived during various periods of immigration. For Polish immigrants, this is especially true because of the vast political and social changes that have taken place in Poland over the past century. One of the strongest links between "old Polonia" and "new Polonia" is sports. This is demonstrated by the creation of various new Polish American sports organizations, particularly the ones which are international in scope. While sports was once the common ground between Polonia and America, it now appears to be the common ground between Old Polonia and New Polonia, and between Polonia and Poland. And though its role is changing, it continues to be a vital force in the ongoing evolution of Polonia.

APPENDIX

National Polish American Sports Hall of Fame Honor Roll

The following is a listing of persons who have been inducted into the National Polish American Sports Hall of Fame, by year of induction.

1973

Stan Musial - "Stan the Man" compiled a .331 career batting average in 22 seasons (1941-63), all with the St. Louis Cardinals. He set numerous team, National League and major league records. He won seven batting titles, including a career-high .376 in 1948. Musial won Most Valuable Player honors in 1943, 1946 and 1948.

1974

Stella (Walasiewicz) Walsh - Polish-born Stella Walsh was one of the greatest woman athletes and held 61 world and national track and field records. She won gold in the 1932 Olympics, and silver in the '36 Games.

Ted Kluszewski - "Big Klu" was a powerful slugger who hit .300 seven times and still carried a lifetime batting average of .301. In 1954, he led the league with 49 home runs and 141 RBI's. Starting in 1951, he led National League first basemen in fielding for five straight years—a major league-record.

Ed (Tyranski) Tyson - Considered one of the softball greats, Ed Tyson starred for Detroit's famed Briggs Beautyware teams. In 1952, he established an Amateur Softball Association World Tournament batting record of .615.

1975

Tony (Zaleski) Zale - Won the World Middleweight Boxing Championship in 1940, lost it to Rocky Graziano, and then regained it in 1948. The "Man of Steel" is considered by many to be the best middleweight ever.

Alex Wojciechowicz - "Alex the Great" was one of Fordham University's legendary "Seven Blocks of Granite" in the late 1930s. A number one draft pick of the Detroit Lions in 1938, he starred as center on offense and linebacker on defense. He was later traded to Philadelphia and played on a pair of NFL champions with the Eagles.

Al (Szymanski) Simmons - Using his unique batting stance, "Bucketfoot Al" had a .334 lifetime batting average. One of the great sluggers of the 1920s and 1930s, he won the Most Valuable Player Award in 1929 and led the American League in 1930 and 1931, hitting .381 and .390 respectively.

1976

Stan (Kowalewski) Coveleski - "Silent Stan" used the then-legal spitball to achieve a 215-142 lifetime record. The right-handed pitcher twice led the American League in Earned Run Average in 1923 and 1925. He had a remarkable World Series for Cleveland in 1920, winning three games against Brooklyn while allowing a total of 2 runs.

John (Krzyminski) Crimmins - For four decades he was a top bowler, winning nearly 100 major tournaments. He won the first National All-Star Bowling tournament in Chicago in 1941.

Ted Marchibroda - A top collegiate quarterback with St. Bonaventure and then the University of Detroit, he led the nation in total offense with 1,813 yards in 1952. He played professionally for four years before launching a very successful coaching career in the NFL.

1977

Bill Osmanski - Dr. William Osmanski starred for the 1937 undefeated Holy Cross football team. He delayed his career as a dentist to play for the Chicago Bears and led the NFL in rushing as a rookie in 1939.

Tom Gola - He was a four-time All-America at LaSalle University from 1952-55 and played on NIT and NCAA championship teams. One of the first big guards in pro basketball at 6-foot-6-inches, he played on an NBA champion with the Philadelphia Warriors.

1978

Johnny (Luczak) Lujack - An All-America quarterback who led Notre Dame to three national titles, Lujack won numerous honors in 1947, including the coveted Heisman Trophy and the Associated Press Athlete of the Year Award. He enjoyed a successful pro career with Chicago.

Eddie (Lopatynski) Lopat - "Steady Eddie" kept hitters off stride with his assortment of slow breaking pitches and had a 166-112 lifetime record. He starred for the great Yankees teams of the late 40s and early 50s and had a 4-1 record in World Series play. In 1951, he won a career-high 21 games and led the American League in Earned Run Average with 2.42.

Ed Lubanski - A top tournament bowler, he won the 1958 World Invitational. In 1959, he captured four ABC titles and was named Bowler of the Year.

1979

Al (Watras) Watrous - A top golfer in the 1920s, Watrous won the Canadian Open in 1922. He also competed on the seniors circuit and won the U.S. Senior Pro Championship three times in the 1950s.

Bill Mazeroski - "The King of Second Basemen" was the best fielder ever at his position, winning eight Gold Gloves Awards and setting numerous records. He hit .260 over his career, .308 in post-season play, and is best known for his dramatic World Series-winning home run in 1960.

Norbert (Szymanski) Schemansky - Record-setting weight-lifter who won two golds, a silver and two bronzes in Olympic competition between 1948 and 1964. He is considered one of the greatest strength athletes of his era.

1980

Bill Skowron - "Moose" Skowron played in the major leagues for 14 seasons (1954-1967), hitting .282 with 211 home runs. He had some clutch World Series hits for the Yankees and then helped beat his former team in the 1963 Series after he was traded to Los Angeles.

Zygmont Czarobski - "Ziggy" earned All-America honors as a defensive tackle for Notre Dame's undefeated national championship team in 1947. The colorful Chicago native also enjoyed a successful pro career.

Robert Gutkowski - Occidental College's internationally known pole-vaulter of the 1950s won a silver medal in the 1956 Olympics. He died in an automobile accident in 1960.

1981

Steve Gromek - He won 123 games and lost 108 in 17 years of major league service with Detroit and Cleveland. After pitching mostly in relief for the '48 Indians, he threw a complete-game 2-1 victory in the pivotal game 4 against the Braves.

Billy Golembiewski - "Billy G" was a star bowler of the 1950s and 1960s despite standing just 5-foot-8 inches tall. He won the American Bowling Congress Masters championship in 1960 and 1962.

Frank (Pajkowski) Parker - One of tennis' unsung greats, the Milwaukee native ranked among the top ten U.S. tennis players for 17 consecutive years (1933-49). His numerous titles included the U.S. Singles Championship in 1943 and 1945.

1982

Tony Kubek - Earned the American League Rookie of the Year Award in 1957 by hitting .297. He became the Yankees' regular shortstop the following year and was a mainstay of some great New York teams. A serious neck and back problem caused him to retire at age 29, after which he began a very successful broadcasting career.

John Payak - An outstanding collegiate guard at Bowling Green in the 1940s, he played professionally with Philadelphia and Milwaukee. He went on to serve as a basketball referee for 17 years in collegiate and tournament play.

Edward Klewicki - A star defensive end at Michigan State, he played professionally with the Detroit Lions. He was a member of the 1935 Lions NFL Championship team.

Edmund Browalski - The founder of the National Polish American Sports Hall of Fame and a sports columnist for over 40 years with the Polish Daily News.

1983

Ron Perranoski - An ace relief pitcher of the 60s and 70s, he posted a 16-3 record with a 1.67 earned run average for the Dodgers in 1963. The Michigan State grad retired with 179 saves and a 2.79 lifetime ERA.

Stanley (Cyganiewicz) Zybyszko - The native of Poland won the world wrestling championship in Philadelphia in 1925. The internationally acclaimed strongman retired at age sixty with more than a thousand victories to his credit.

Ann Setlock - A top women's bowler who set numerous Michigan records, including a 776 set. She was a member of WIBC championship teams in 1957 and 1959.

Warren Orlick - Known internationally as golf's "Mr. Rules," he was a golf professional for over fifty years. He was named Pro Golfer of the Year in 1960.

1984

Vince Boryla - An All-America at Notre Dame and Denver University, he was a member of the gold medal-winning 1948 U.S. Olympic Basketball team. He went on to pro basketball success as a player, coach and general manager.

Cass Grygier - He began bowling in 1926 and rolled his first 300 game in his first year of play. He was a member of the Detroit Stroh's team that won an American Bowling Congress Tournament title, and won the International Doubles Title in Berlin in 1936.

Stanley (Kiecal) Ketchel - "The Michigan Assassin" won the Middleweight Boxing Championship in 1908. Although he was shot to death in 1910 at the age of 24, he is considered one of the division's greatest champions.

1985

Hank (Wilczek) Stram - The Gary, Indiana, native was one of pro football's most successful and innovative coaches. His Dallas Texans won the 1962 AFL title, and his Kansas City Chiefs won Super Bowl IV in 1970.

George Szypula - A star gymnast at Temple University, he went on to coach the sport at Michigan State. His athletes have won numerous NCAA and Big Ten titles, and the Spartans captured the NCAA Championship in 1958.

1986

Dick Modzelewski - "Big Mo" won the Outland Trophy as college football's top defensive lineman in 1952 with the University of Maryland. He went on to an outstanding 14-year NFL career, including playing for championship teams with New York (1956) and Cleveland (1964).

Carl Yastrzemski - For twenty-three years "Yaz" performed for the Boston Red Sox, collecting 3,419 hits, 1,844 runs batted in, and 452 home runs. He was the last man to win baseball's "Triple Crown" in 1967 when he led the American League in hitting (.326), homers (44) and RBIs (121).

1987

Jack Ham - The Penn State All-America enjoyed a 12-year career with the Pittsburgh Steelers, earning All-Pro honors nine straight years. He played in four Super Bowl Champions.

Vic Janowicz - The Ohio State triple threat won the Heisman Trophy in 1950. He played both baseball and football professionally before a near-fatal automobile accident in 1956 ended his athletic career.

Bob (Algustoski) Toski - One of the smallest men (125-pounds) to star on the pro golf tour, he won four major tournaments in 1954. He also competed on the Senior Tour. This son of Polish immigrants became one of golf's leading teaching pros and authored three books on the sport.

1988

Leon Hart - The talented end starred on three national championship Notre Dame football teams in the 1940s and won the 1949 Heisman Trophy. He had an All-Pro career with the Detroit Lions, playing on three NFL championship squads.

George "Whitey" Kurowski - Despite a childhood accident that made his right arm shorter than his left, Kurowski starred for the St. Louis Cardinals from 1941 to 1949. The three-time All-Star was an outstanding third baseman and a .286 career hitter.

Billy (Paczkowski) Packer- After a fine collegiate playing and coaching career, he became a basketball color commentator in 1972. He went on to work many national broadcasts, earning a reputation as one of the most knowledgeable and outspoken broadcasters in the business.

1989

Greg Luzinski - "The Bull" played in the major leagues for thirteen years with the Phillies and White Sox. The four-time All-Star knocked in 307 homers and 1,128 runs.

Frank Gatski - "Gunner" played in 11 championship games during his 12-year pro career and came out on the winning side in eight of them. Considered football's greatest center of the 1950s, he played most of his career with Cleveland before finishing his NFL career with Detroit.

1990

Phil Niekro - His baffling knuckleball helped him become just the 19th pitcher in major league history to win 300 games. "Knucksie" garnered 318 wins in 24 seasons before retiring at age 48.

Janet Lynn (Nowicki) - She won five consecutive U.S. Women's National Skating Championships and was a bronze medalist at the 1972 Olympics. Janet signed a $1.45 million contract with the Ice Follies, but severe asthma attacks caused her to end her pro career.

Pete Banaszak - A "lunch bucket" running back for the Oakland Raiders, he ran for 3,767 yards and caught passes for

1,022 yards during his 13-year NFL career. He was known for his effectiveness in short-yardage situations and scored 52 touchdowns.

1991

Ron Jaworski - "The Polish Rifle" played pro football for seventeen years, mostly with the Philadelphia Eagles, passing for 28,190 yards and 179 touchdowns. In 1980, he was named NFL Player of the Year for leading the Eagles to the NFC title.

Mike Krzyzewski - One of the most highly regarded coaches in college basketball, Krzyzewski led the Duke basketball team to consecutive NCAA titles in 1991 and 1992. His Blue Devils have enjoyed a period of dominance unprecedented in the modern era.

Stanley Stanczyk - This Detroit native won the first of six consecutive world titles in weightlifting in 1946. He won gold in the '48 Olympics and silver in the '52 Games.

1992

Dan Abramowicz - Not highly regarded coming out of college, Abramowicz enjoyed an outstanding nine-year NFL career. The sure-handed receiver set a record for catching at least one pass in 105 straight games (1967-1974) and led the league in receiving in 1969 with 73 catches for 1,015 yards.

Joe Niekro - He enjoyed a 22-year major league career winning 221 games, mostly with the Houston Astros. Joe and brother Phil combined for 539 pitching victories, more than any other brother combination in major league history.

Tom Paciorek - Paciorek started out as a member of the Hamtramck, Michigan, 1961 Pony Baseball League World Champions and then was an All-America outfielder and highly rated defensive back at the University of Houston. He then embarked on an 18-year major league baseball career, first languishing in the Dodgers system. He blossomed as a player when he signed with Seattle in 1978, and hit a career-high .326 for the Mariners in 1981.

1993

Steve Bartkowski - The first player chosen in the 1975 NFL draft following an All-America career at California, "Bart" starred for the Atlanta Falcons for eleven years. Considered the prototype NFL quarterback, he threw for 24,122 yards and 156 touchdowns in his pro career.

Len Ceglarski - When he retired in 1992 after thirty-four years of coaching, he was the most winning coach in the history of college hockey. He picked up most of his 673 wins with Boston College, where he only had three losing seasons out of twenty.

Jim Grabowski - An All-America running back at the University of Illinois, Grabowski broke many school rushing records held by Red Grange. He was named Big Ten Most Valuable Player, as well as MVP in the Fighting Illini's 1964 Rose Bowl triumph. He was a number one pick of the Green Bay Packers in 1966, but a promising pro career was cut short by a serious knee injury.

1994

Carol Blazejowski - "Blaze" scored 3,199 points during her four-year basketball career at Montclair State, for an average of 31.7 points a game, a women's record that still stands. She was a three-time All-America and captain of the 1980 Olympic team.

Lou (Majka) Michaels - A two-time All-America defensive lineman at the University of Kentucky, he went on to a thirteen-year NFL career as a defensive end. He kicked for 955 points as well, retiring in 1971 as the NFL's fourth all-time leading scorer.

Dick Szymanski - A four-year starter at Notre Dame, "Syzzie" was a linebacker for the 1953 national championship team.

The versatile center/linebacker played for thirteen years with the Baltimore Colts and played on three championship teams. After retiring as a player, he held various positions with the Colts front office, including general manager.

1995

Zeke Bratkowski -Edmund "Zeke" Bratkowski played football for the University of Georgia, leading the NCAA in passing yards in 1952. He played professionally for the Bears, Rams and Packers. He was best-known as Bart Starrs back-up in Green Bay and played an important role on the great Packer teams of the mid-1960s. After his fourteen-year pro-playing career, he became one of the most respected offensive coaches in the NFL.

Barney McCosky - Considered one of baseball's top leadoff hitters of the 1940s, the speedy outfielder led the Detroit Tigers to the pennant in 1940 when he hit .340 with 39 doubles and 19 triples. Military service shortened his career and a severe back injury hampered his effectiveness in later years, but McCosky was still able to post an impressive .312 lifetime batting average.

Frank Szymanski -The former All-State football player at Detroit's Northeastern High School played center for the 1943 national championship Notre Dame football team. He went on to a successful pro career and played for the 1949 NFL champion Philadelphia Eagles. He later served as probate judge of Wayne County (Michigan) for nearly twenty years.

*   *   *

The National Polish American Sports Hall of Fame Museum is located on the campus of St. Mary's College in Orchard Lake, Michigan, about 25 miles northwest of Detroit. The museum is located on the second floor of the Dombrowski Fieldhouse, and tours can be arranged by calling (313) 683-0401.

Any male or female athlete of Polish American extraction (father or mother must be Polish) and meeting eligibility criteria may be considered. All amateur athletes are eligible. Collegiate athletes not continuing into the professional ranks are eligible two years after their college participation ends. Professional athletes (except those competing in a seniors division) are eligible two years after their retirement.

The NPASHFM is a member of the International Association of Sports Museums and Halls of Fame, and contributions are tax-deductible as provided under IRS regulation 501(c)(3).

Nominations for the National Polish American Sports Hall of Fame can be sent to: 11445 Conant, Hamtramck, MI 48212.

BIBLIOGRAPHY

BOOKS

Bukowczyk, John J. *And My Children Did Not Know Me: A History of the Polish Americans*. Bloomington and Indianapolis: Indiana University Press, 1987.

Daly, Dan and O'Donnell, Bob. *Pro Football Chronicle*. New York: Collier Press, 1990.

Davies, Norman. *Gods Playground: A History of Poland*. New York: Columbia University Press, 1982.

Fleischer, Nat. *The Michigan Assassin*. New York:C.J. OBrien, 1946.

Gella, Aleksander. *Development of Class Structure in Eastern Europe*. Albany: State University of New York Press, 1989.

Grabowski, John J. *Sports In Cleveland*. Bloomington and Indianapolis: Indiana University Press, 1992.

Gregorich, Barbara. *Women At Play: The Story of Women in Baseball*. New York: Harcourt Brace & Co., 1993.

Gretzky, Walter and Taylor, Jim. *Gretzky: From the Back Yard Rink to the Stanley Cup*. New York: Avon Books, 1985.

Gretzky, Wayne with Rick Reilly. *Gretzky: An Autobiography*. New York: Harper Collins, 1990.

James, Bill. *The Bill James Historical Abstract*. New York: Villard Books, 1988.

Johnson, Jack. *Jack Johnson in the Ring and Out*. Chicago: National Sports Publications, 1927.

Klecko, Joe, Fields, Joe and Logan, Greg. *Nose To Nose: Survival in the Trenches of the NFL*. New York: William Morrow & Co., 1989.

Koppett, Leonard. *24 Seconds to Shoot: An Informal History of the National Basketball Association*. New York: Macmillan, 1968.

Kubek, Tony and Pluto, Terry. *Sixty-One: The Team, The Record, The Men*. New York: Macmillan, 1987.

Kuniczak, W.S. *My Name is Million*. Garden City, New York: Doubleday & Co., 1978.

Lansche, Jerry. *Stan The Man Musial: Born to Be a Ballplayer*. Dallas:

Taylor Publishing Co., 1994.

Levine, Peter. *Ellis Island to Ebbets Field: Sport and the American Jewish Experience*. New York: Oxford University Press, 1992.

Macy, Sue. *A Whole New Ball Game*. New York: Henry Hull & Co., 1993.

Musial, Stan as told to Broeg, Bob. *Stan Musial: "The Man's" Own Story*. Garden City, New York: Doubleday & Co., 1964.

McFarlane, Brian. *The Story of the National Hockey League*. New York: Charles Scribner's Sons, 1973.

Niekro, Phil and Joe, with Picking, Ken. *The Niekro Files*. Chicago: Contemporary Books, 1988.

Odd, Gilbert. *Encyclopedia of Boxing*. New York: Crescent Books, 1983.

Packer, Billy with Lazenby, Roland. *Hoops! Confessions of a College Basketball Analyst*. Chicago: Contemporary Books, 1986.

Peterson, Robert W. *Cages To Jump Shots: Pro Basketball's Early Years*. New York, Oxford: Oxford University Press, 1990.

Peterson, William, Novak, Michael, and Gleason, Philip. *Concepts of Ethnicity*. Cambridge, Massachusetts: The Belknap Press of Harvard University Press, 1980.

Sowell, Thomas. *Ethnic America*. New York: Basic Books, Inc., 1981.

Shatzin, Mike, ed.. *The Ballplayers*. New York: Arbor House William Morrow & Co., 1990.

Stram, Hank with Sahadi, Lou, *They're Playing My Game*. New York: William Morrow & Co., 1986.

Thomas, William I. and Znaniecki, Florian. *The Polish Peasant in Europe and America*. New York: Alfred A. Knopf, 1927.

Twombly, Wells. *Shake Down the Thunder*! Radnor PA: Chilton Book Co., 1987.

Waldo, Artur L. *First Poles in America 1608-1958*. Pittsburgh: Polish Falcons of America, 1956.

Weyand, Alexander M., *The Cavalcade of Basketball*. New York: Macmillan, 1960.

Willoughby, David P. *The Super Athletes*. Cranbury NJ: A.S. Barnes & Co., 1970.

Wolff, Rick, ed. *The Baseball Encyclopedia*. New York: Macmillian, 1993.

Wytrywal, Joseph A. *America's Polish Heritage: A Social History of Poles in America*. Detroit: Endurance Press, 1961.

Wytrywal, Joseph A. *Behold! The Polish-Americans*. Detroit:

Endurance Press, 1977.

Yastrzemski, Carl and Eskenazi, Gerald. *Yaz: Baseball, the Wall and Me.* New York: Doubleday, 1990.

Yastrzemski, Carl with Hirshberg, Al. *Yaz.* New York: Viking Press, 1968.

NEWSPAPERS

Buffalo, NY: *Am-Pol Eagle, Courier-Express, Buffalo News*
Chicago, IL: *Chicago Tribune*
Cleveland, OH: *Plain Dealer*
Detroit, MI: *Detroit Free Press*
Grand Rapids, MI: *Grand Rapids Press*
Los Angeles CA: *Los Angeles Times, Los Angeles Herald Examine*
New York, NY: *New York Evening Journal, New York Post, New York Times*
Polish American Journal
Polish American World
Polish Daily News

MAGAZINES

College Sports
Inside Sports
People Magazine
Ring Magazine
Sporting News
Sports Illustrated

INDEX OF NAMES

INDEX OF NAMES

POLISH HISTORY & BIOGRAPHY

THE FORGOTTEN FEW: The Polish Air Force in the Second World War
Adam Zamoyski, 272 pages, 30 illustrations, 3 maps, $24.95 hardcover, 0-7818-0421-3
Winston Churchill speaking about the Battle of Britain in 1940 said: "Never was so much owed by so many to so few." This is the story of some of the few who are rarely remembered by our Allies today.
Some 17,000 men and women passed through the ranks of the Polish Air Force while it was stationed on British soil in World War II. They not only played a crucial role in the Battle of Britain in 1940, they also contributed significantly to the Allied war effort in the air. This is the story of who they were, where they came from and what they did. Adam Zamoyski is the author of many books on Poland, including the much acclaimed *Polish Way*.

CASIMIR PULASKI: A Hero of the American Revolution
Leszek Szymanski, Ph.D. Foreword by Brig. Gen. Thaddeus Maliszewski, $24.95 hardcover, maps, 300 pages, 0-7818-0157-5
There has been no authoritative, documented biography - readily available to readers and researchers - of Pulaski's American years. The man who was willing to: "hazard all for the freedom of America" did not live to tell his own story. This thorough, meticulously researched, and objective book will set the record straight.

PILSUDSKI - A LIFE FOR POLAND
Waclaw Jedrzejewicz. Introduction by Zbigniew Brzezinski. $11.95 paperback, illustrated, 0-87052-747-9
A masterly biography of the man who personified his country's desire for true autonomy, written by Pilsudski's longtime collaborator and eminent scholar.
"An important study, a very useful book. *-Choice*
"A pleasure to read." *-Perspectives*

THE POLISH WAY: A THOUSAND-YEAR HISTORY OF THE POLES AND THEIR CULTURE

Adam Zamoyski, $18.95 paperback, 422 pages, 170 illustrations, 0-7818-0200-8
"Zamoyski strives to place Polish history more squarely in its European context, and he pays special attention to developments that had repercussions beyond the boundaries of the country. For example, he emphasizes the phenomenon of the Polish parliamentary state in Central Europe, its spectacular 16th century success and its equally spectacular disintegration two centuries later...This is popular history at its best, neither shallow nor simplistic...lavish illustrations, good maps and intriguing charts and genealogical tables make this book particularly attractive." -*Piotr Wandycz, Professor of European History, Yale University in the New York Times Book Review.*

STEEL WILL: The Life of Tad Sendzimir

Vanda Sendzimir. $24.95 hardcover, 520 pages, 0-7818-0169-9
One of the world's greatest inventors and entrepreneurs, Tad Sendzimir's innovations in steel-making lie behind many of the great technological developments of the last sixty years, from war-time radar to the space program.
Stefan Bratkowski, Poland's premier journalist who had known Sendzimir, writes in his review of the book: "The book should be a part of every Polish-American library; it is a handbook of courage and aspirations for young people, a testimony of Polish contribution and a source of great pride for older generations. The book should be a present for American friends, because there is no steel factory in America which could succeed without Sendzimir's inventions. I wish it a success worthy of its hero."

DID THE CHILDREN CRY?
Hitler's War Against Jewish and Polish Children, 1939-1945

Richard C. Lukas, $24.95 hardcover, 320 pages, photos, 0-7818-0242-3
Based on eyewitness accounts, interviews and prodigious research by the author, this is a unique and most compelling account of German inhumanity to children in occupied Poland. An unprecedented aspect of Nazi genocide in World War II was their brutal and deliberate decision not to spare the children. Jewish children, first driven into ghettos, were marked for total destruction once 'The Final Solution' was put into action. Gentile children were starved, killed or Germanized in order to reduce the Polish nation to a small complement of semi-literate slaves tending the Herrenvolk in their thousand-year Reich.
"While this account does not diminish the unique place Jewish children had in the scale of suffering, it also does not downplay the tragedy experienced by Polish children."-*Shofar*

CLASSICS FROM POLISH LITERATURE

QUO VADIS?
Henryk Sienkiewicz, 470 pages, $14.95 paperback, 0-7818-0185-1; Also available in hardcover, $22.50, 0-7818-0100-0
"In a new American translation by Rev. Stanley F. Conrad, Poland's - and the world's - greatest bestseller comes alive for a new generation of readers. Powerful in its message of Christ's and His Apostles' teaching, Father Conrad's work is literally and spiritually faithful to Sienkiewicz's original Polish prose." -*The Polish Advocate*

IN DESERT AND WILDERNESS
by Nobel Prize Winner Henryk Sienkiewicz, translated by Miroslaw Lipinski. 278 pages, $19.95 cloth, 0-7818-0235-0
The story, a perennial bestseller in Poland, is anchored in an authentic episode of African history when the followers of Mohammed Ahmed (known as 'Mahdi'), leader of an Islamic crusade, defeated the British in the siege of Khartoum in 1884. The adventures of Stas Tarkowski, a Polish boy of fourteen, and eight-year old Nell Rawlinson, his English friend, their kidnapping by the followers of Mahdi, and their successful escape and return to their parents, have captivated readers young and old for a century.
The full color cover illustration is by Tadeusz Styka, a famous painter and illustrator.

PAN TADEUSZ (bilingual edition)
Adam Mickiewicz. Polish and English text side by side. Translated by Kenneth R. MacKenzie. $19.95 paperback, 600 pages, 0-7818-0033-1
Poland's greatest epic poem is now available in North America in what is its finest translation. *Pan Tadeusz* is a tale of country life among the Polish and Lithuanian gentry in the years 1811 and 1812. For American students of Polish, and for Polish students of English, this classic poem in simultaneous translation embodies the ideals, the sentiments, and the way of life of a whole nation, lending to its universal and timeless appeal.

THE LITTLE TRILOGY

By Nobel Prize Winner Henryk Sienkiewicz, translated by Miroslaw Lipinski.
$19.95 cloth, 267 pages, 0-7818-0293-8

Now available for the first time in one volume are three memorable Sienkiewicz stories - "The Old Servant," "Hania," and "Selim Mirza" - collected to tell a venerable tale of love, honor and glory. In Poland, these stories (two are lengthy novellas) are referred to as "The Little Trilogy" because they portray so splendidly the same cast of characters found in *The Trilogy*.

In a new translation by Miroslaw Lipinski, *The Little Trilogy* contains everything readers have come to expect of the celebrated Sienkiewicz - charming and alluring characters, romance, heart-break, action and adventure, humor and bravery.

OUR POLISH HERITAGE BESTSELLERS

TREASURY OF POLISH LOVE POEMS, QUOTATIONS & PROVERBS
In Polish & English side by side.

Now in Audiocassette...
hardback: Miroslaw Lipinski, editor. $11.95 cloth, 128 pages, 0-7818-0297-0
audiobook: 2 cassettes, approx. 1 hour running time, $12.95, 0-7818-0361-6
This handsome bilingual collection of over 100 works by 44 of Poland's prominent authors, each represented by one or two of their poems, reflects the best of Polish love. Authors include Jan Kochanowski, Adam Mickiewicz, Konstanty Ildefons Galczynski, Jan Andrzej Morsztyn and Julian Tuwim. These elegant editions will be a treasured gift for lovers of all ages and a wonderful way to learn Polish or English.
In the audiobook, poems, quotations and proverbs are read in Polish and English, providing language students with an instant translation of each Polish selection. The Polish portions of the cassettes are read by members of the Cracow Artistic Ensemble. English portions are read by Ken Kliban, an actor with Broadway credits and extensive narrating experience.

POLISH HERITAGE COOKERY
Robert and Maria Strybel. $35.00 hardcover, 882 pages, with line drawing, 0-7818-0069-2
"An encyclopedia of Polish cookery and a wonderful thing to have." *-Julia Child, ABC's Good Morning America*"
"POLISH HERITAGE COOKERY is well organized, informative, interlaced with historical background on Polish foods and eating habits, with easy-to-follow recipes readily prepared in American kitchens and, above all, it's fun to read." *-Polish American Cultural Network*
"A culinary classic in the making, this comprehensive collection of over 2,200 recipes is by Polonia's most famous chef." *-Zgoda*
"This cookbook is the most extensive and varied one ever published in English." *- Polish Heritage Quarterly*

POLISH CUSTOMS, TRADITIONS, AND FOLKLORE

Sophie Hodorowicz Knab. With an introduction by Rev. Czeslaw Krysa. $19.95 hardcover, 300 pages, 0-7818-0068-4

This unique reference book, now in its third printing, is arranged by month, showing various Polish occasions, feasts and holidays. Line illustrations complete this rich and varied treasury of folklore. Sophie Hodorowicz Knab is the heritage editor for the national *Polish American Journal*, noted lecturer and syndicated writer on folklore. Rev. Krysa, Professor at the S.S. Cyril and Methodius Seminary in Orchard Lake, Michigan, is an authority on Polish folklore.

"A tremendous asset to understanding the ethnic behavior of a people. Highly recommended." *-Polish American Journal*

By the same author....
POLISH HERBS, FLOWERS & FOLK MEDICINE

Sophie Hodorowicz Knab, 252 pages, illustrations, $19.95 hardcover, 0-7818-0319-5

This unique and authentic guide to Polish herbs and flowers essential to the people of Poland takes the reader on a tour of monastery, castle and cottage gardens and provides details on over 100 herbs and flowers and how they were used in folk medicine as well as everyday life, traditions, and customs. Patters of knot gardens and herb gardens from Poland are described along with illustrations and woodcuts.

This book is a volume of history, a how-to guide and a source of inspiration for those who wish to recreate Polish gardens from the past. It includes a list of mail-order nurseries offering herbs and flowers mentioned in this book.

THE POLISH HERITAGE SONGBOOK

Compiled by Marek Sart, illustrated by Szymon Kobylinski, 172 pages, 65 illus., 78 songs, $14.95 paperback, 0-7818-0425-6

This collection of 78 songs is a treasury of nostalgia and an object lesson in Polish history which gives testimony to the indomitable Polish spirit and the national will to be free.

A distinguished musicologist, Stanislaw Werner has written the annotations for the songs, giving a wealth of information about the composers and the librettists as well as the song histories. These texts are in English; the texts of the song's are in Polish.

LANGUAGE INSTRUCTION BOOKS
& DICTIONARIES

POLISH-ENGLISH/ENGLISH-POLISH PRACTICAL DICTIONARY
700 pages, $11.95 paperback, 0-7818-0085-4
This bestselling Polish/English dictionary, now revised, reset and redesigned, features over 31,000 entries and a glossary of menu terms.

POLISH-ENGLISH/ENGLISH-POLISH STANDARD DICTIONARY
780 pages, $19.95 paperback, 0-7818-0282-2
With over 32,000 entries, including irregular verbs, proper names and terms. Completely redesigned and reset.

POLISH-ENGLISH/ENGLISH-POLISH CONCISE DICTIONARY
408 pages, $8.95 paperback, 0-7818-0133-8
In its fourth edition, featuring over 8,000 entries, and complete phonetics. Ideal for travelers and students.

POLISH PHRASEBOOK AND DICTIONARY
225 pages, $9.95 paperback, 0-7818-0134-6
This handy guide for the English speaking traveler is more useful then ever.

BEGINNER'S POLISH
200 pages, $9.95 paperback, 0-7818-0299-7
A modern, up-to-date language instruction guide for students with little or no background in Polish.

HIGHLANDER POLISH-ENGLISH/ENGLISH-HIGHLANDER POLISH DICTIONARY
111 pages, $9.95 paperback, 0-7818-0303-9
"As a proud American of Polish *"goral"* descent, I am delighted that Jan Gutt-Mostowy from Poronin in Podhale, prepared a Polish-Goral-English dictionary. It is obviously a labor of love that will elicit appreciation and recognition and allow the richness and beauty of the *"gwara goralska"* to become more availabe to the English-speaking world."

TO PURCHASE HIPPOCRENE'S BOOKS contact your local bookstore, or write to Hippocrene Books, 171 Madison Avenue, New York, NY 10016. Please enclose a check or money order, adding $5.00 for shipping (UPS) for the first book, and 50 cents for each additional book.
Our complete catalog is available upon request.